An Evil Grows in Pasadena

J. Roswell

PublishAmerica
Baltimore

First printing

ISBN: 1-4137-2860-X
PUBLISHED BY PUBLISHAMERICA, LLLP
www.publishamerica.com
Baltimore

Printed in the United States of America

To my brother, Tim, for his inspiration…

A Note

While Pasadena is a real place, the characters in the story are not, and their actions are strictly fictional. Any relation to true events or real people is not the authors intention as the characters and action are from the author's imagination.

J. Roswell

October

What we anticipate seldom occurs; what we least expected generally happens.

-Henrietta Tempe, B. Disraelli, 1837

One

Sitting on a faded camp chair, Johnnie carefully folded the Sunday paper and laid it on the worn, wood picnic table. She still kept some items from her old life, accumulated before moving into the beautiful home made possible by lucrative residuals from Patrick's textbooks. She sighed, thinking about the dry, Santa Ana heat that came straight from the desert that she and her husband, Patrick, would have to negotiate on the way to a dinner meeting at Lionel Marshall's, a lawyer friend of theirs. They both lived in the Pasadena area in fine, lovely homes.

The large patio landing and old lawn furniture could not be seen from the house, and Johnnie often used it as a retreat. She hadn't as yet had time to do her daily workout because of entertaining their son, Ian, home for a weekend in his first year of college.

Ian had left after the delicious brunch of eggs benedict, grapefruit, and sour cream coffeecake. They was no champagne because Ian was under age and was planning to drive back to school; but they did have the Kona coffee Johnnie's friend, Dee, brought back from her trip to Hawaii. She made the special breakfast even though the only special occasion was that Ian was home.

Johnnie decided to finish her walk down the stairs, then turn around and head up to the top. She'd been sitting on a scenic landing on the long staircase leading to the lower reaches of their extensive property. She wanted to get some exercise in before the dinner meeting as both she and Patrick worked to keep their trim, fit figures. She finished at a brisk pace without stopping to rest on the landing and sped right up to the large lanai. She was pleased with its beautiful furniture of iron and glass; it was a nice contrast with the homey old furniture on the landing.

Once in the cooler house, she headed up the back stairs, pausing on her way to the bathroom to look lovingly at the pictures of her three children, her sons Scott and Ian and her daughter Colleen. She sighed again. Ian attended Occidental College in the area, but since Colleen was a senior at UC Berkeley, she couldn't visit as often. Scott was finished with school and had earned an MBA from UCLA. Now he worked as the President of Aunt Rose's company and had his own apartment. She and Patrick both missed their children but knew that the day would come when the children would go their own ways. Still, a quiet house was hard to get used to after all of the kids' activities that had filled their home for so many years.

Johnnie needed to hurry up as she realized that time was starting to get away from her. She intended to take a relaxing bubble bath to prepare herself for the evening. They were to get a presentation on a moneymaking proposition at Lionel's. Although they now had plenty of money because of Patrick's history textbooks, they were still interested.

Before getting into the tub, Johnnie put some music on their new state of the art sound system to help her relax. The house had needed some work when they bought it, but not much because they were only the second family to own the home. Just the kitchen and bathrooms needed to be brought up to date, which they did in a very tasteful way. None of the rooms were jarring. They did try to keep the feel of the 1920s house.

This restoration work was exciting for both Johnnie and Patrick. They'd enjoyed it so much that, when they had the chance, they'd bought another piece of property in the Oak Glen area that had a fixer-up building on it. They had big plans for the property and were looking forward to the next year when they'd be able to start work on their new home.

But for now, Patrick was busy working on a revision of one of his textbooks. The original book had been adopted as a textbook for colleges and universities around the country. He and his co-authors, fellow history professors, had done very well with the original, now they were trying to repeat the success with the revision. The money from the revision, assuming its success, would be needed to implement the plans for the Oak Glen property. Maybe Lionel's proposition would let them move forward ahead of schedule.

After soaking in her bubble bath, Johnnie got dressed in a hurry. She applied subtle evening makeup, just making up her eyes and using a little blush. She took good care of her beautiful skin and never wore much makeup. She fixed her sandy blond hair in an upsweep, fastened it with a sparkling clip, and added small sparkling earrings. The outfit she chose was a silk pajama-type outfit, green with a little blue pattern, which made her hazel eyes more green than blue.

"You look stunning, Mrs. Collins," Patrick gushed when her saw her, enfolding her in a big hug and dropping several sweet kisses on her lips.

He was dressed in an exquisitely tailored dark blue suit that set his blue eyes off nicely. He was trim and taller than Johnnie, though they both had sandy blonde hair and similar features. Patrick called them bookends.

"Thank you, you handsome devil," Johnnie replied as she squeezed Patrick's hand back.

"How are your shoes? I thought we would walk to Lionel's house. We won't be able to park much closer than here anyway," Patrick said, checking his wife's feet.

"I think these shoes will do okay," Johnnie said. "I didn't wear my high, high heels for this affair. After all, we probably will be standing a lot. I do hope that Lionel will have seating when we listen to the presentation. And this better not be a moneymaker that involves all of us selling stuff."

"Oh, we don't have to worry about that. Lionel wouldn't dare ask any of us to sell anything. It'll probably be an investment in something that's supposed to have good returns." Patrick straightened his tie and took Johnnie's arm, "It's getting late, let's go."

Out on the sidewalk the two strolled causally but briskly, holding hands in the twilight as they went. They made a striking picture of a tall handsome man and beautiful woman. As they walked, they talked quietly.

"Did I tell you that not only are you very beautiful but you smell nice too?" Patrick cooed, squeezing her hand as he spoke. Johnnie squeezed his hand in reply. With that, they arrived at Lionel's expansive house. The one-story ranch house was newer than the Collins' two-story twenties home. It was long across the front and stretched out in an L on both sides. The Collins joked that to really get around in that house one needed roller skates. The façade was a gray stone with darker gray stucco. Lionel's wife, Linda, had the front door painted a dark mauve and the trim was in dark gray with mauve highlights. The roof was low and dark. The gardens in front provided a lot of color. In the spring, the azaleas were a profusion of pinks and reds and were spectacular. For fall, mums were planted in golds, oranges, and white. As Johnnie and Patrick walked up the stone walkway, they admired the landscaping as they always did.

Two

"Mr. and Mrs. Collins," said Lionel as he swung the door open before they even had a chance to ring the bell. There he stood, a tall man, handsome in a distinguished way, with his dark hair graying at the temples. He wore a deep gray suit with a pale lavender shirt and dark paisley print silk tie. As he bent his head in a slight bow the little bald spot on the back of his head shined in the setting sun.

After they got over the door flying open so suddenly, Patrick shook Lionel's hand and Johnnie said a cheery hello as she quickly maneuvered past her host, avoiding one of his wet kisses.

"Let me introduce our guest of honor, then could you two introduce him to the others? I'm alone this evening," Lionel asked once they were in the large foyer of his rambling house.

"We would be happy to, Lionel. Where is Linda this evening?" Johnnie replied, puzzled.

"Oh, she had something she needed to take care of out of town," Lionel mumbled vaguely.

The three of them walked into the large sunken living room in thoughtful silence. A man was standing, gazing out the picture windows at the end of the living room. The windows looked out on an even more beautiful backyard that included a swimming pool and a bed of roses behind it.

"Dr. and Mrs. Collins, I would like you to meet Mr. Charles Edward Defoe, Jr. And Mr. Defoe, I would like you to meet Dr. and Mrs. Collins," Lionel said.

"Please call me Patrick, Mr. Defoe," Patrick offered, shaking Charles's hand.

"And please, call me Johnnie," Johnnie added as Charles took her

15

hands in his holding her hands firm but soft at the same time.

"I'm so pleased to meet both of you," Charles said in a voice of honey, while gazing deeply into Johnnie's hazel eyes. "And please call me Charles."

Charles was an amazing man. He was not what one would call movie-star handsome but rather had good, even looks. His thick, light brown hair was neatly parted and combed without a hair out of place. His dark suit was as exquisitely tailored as Patrick's. He wore a diamond stud for a tie tack on his very conservative tie, set off by a red rose bud with baby's breath on his lapel. He wasn't as tall as Patrick; but he stood very straight. He oozed confidence even though he would be younger by some years than the youngest guest at the party.

"Here's the guest list. Maybe you could go over it and explain who these people are to Charles so that introductions will go faster," Lionel asked, handing the list to Johnnie. "I have to see about some details about the party. I sure appreciate your help. By the way would you please get the door when the people come? That would really help too."

"Well, okay, I'll see what I can do and Patrick can help too. Charles, Patrick, let's sit over here," Johnnie said.

Johnnie led them over to one of the long, low, fifties sofas. The room was done in a modern theme. Johnnie was glad she had on long pants when she sat down because a skirt would have been hard to handle. She was puzzled by Lionel's strange behavior. *Where was Linda? Were Linda and Lionel in the midst of getting a divorce and the great divorce lawyer was too embarrassed to admit to it? Why were they being treated like co-hosts?*

"So, do you want me to start?" Patrick said to break the silence.

"Yes, you go ahead, dear," Johnnie said distracted.

As the two men talked over her, Johnnie only half listened as she continued to try to puzzle out what was happening. This was truly turning out to be a strange evening. The doorbell brought Johnnie back to the present, and she rose from the sofa and went to answer the door. There were professors Robert James, Neal Smythe, and

Thornton Wallace of The High Notes combo. The men all were smiling some of their biggest smiles on seeing Johnnie but no one grinned as big or hard as Neal Smythe who had a well-known crush on her.

"Hello, Mrs. Collins, Johnnie, that is, do you know where Lionel wants us to set up?" Thornton Wallace served as both the piano player and leader of the combo since he was the only professor of music in the group, the others being from the history department.

"You're to set up in the solarium to the side of the bar. I think it will become clear when you get there. Have you played here before?"

"Yes, we've played here for several functions. But this time we are to attend the meeting. Do you know anything about it?"

"Only that it will be a moneymaking proposition and only a few people are invited. Lionel is not available right now but I know he could answer your questions," Johnnie said.

"Well, guys, let's get our equipment set up. This party starts at five o'clock and it's four-twenty now, so we don't have much time," Thornton said to the other combo members. "Johnnie, would you show me exactly where we should set up?"

Johnnie showed Thornton where to go while she puzzled about why she and Patrick were told the party started at four p.m. In fact, Lionel had been quite insistent that they be there precisely at four o'clock.

When the High Notes brought their equipment in, Johnnie smiled to herself being careful to keep a straight face. Neal Smythe made quit a picture as the short, dumpy man struggled to carry in his bass fiddle. Thornton came in carrying the large keyboard he used when there wasn't a piano available. Last came Robert carrying his sax and whatever else he could manage that they would need. Once Robert entered, the High Notes began to set up and Johnnie went back to find her Patrick and Charles.

She found the men where she had left them, deep in conversation, laughing and talking. Both men stood as Johnnie entered the room.

"We covered this list Lionel left pretty thoroughly," Patrick said, taking Johnnie's hand.

17

"Yes, I feel like I know everyone now and am looking forward to meeting them face to face. Thanks for the help."

"There's the doorbell, I think that might be guests as it is close to five," Johnnie said checking her watch.

"Johnnie, do you know where Lionel is?" Patrick asked. "I suppose we better answer that door if he isn't around."

"I haven't seen Lionel for a while now, so I'll answer the door. Why don't you take Charles to the solarium where the bar and the High Notes are? I'll send the people back to you," Johnnie said over her shoulder as she headed for the continually ringing doorbell.

"Oh, hello, Johnnie Collins, where are Lionel and Linda?" a gruff voice asked.

"Hello to you too, Bill Carmichael, and you too, Betty. Linda is out of town, so Lionel asked me to answer the door. Just go to the solarium where Patrick will introduce you to the speaker for this evening," Johnnie said.

Bill Carmichael was a nice neighbor, but a little rough around the edges. He owned B&B Services, a company that did industrial cleaning and steam cleaning of parking lots. It was hard work but he made very good money from his business. He made a meaty presence in his dark suit with his pale pink dress shirt. His wife Betty, in her earth-tone printed pantsuit, was little and cute in a pixie sort of way. They really made an odd couple but loved each other very much.

Following right on the heels of the Carmichaels was the widow Anna Malloy, a neighbor who was older than the rest of the partygoers. Her only daughter lived in New York with her husband and three children. Anna didn't see much of her family because she lived so far away. With this opportunity, Anna hoped to earn enough to travel back East to see her daughter and grandchildren more often.

Stan and Barb Stevens from across the street were next. Barb was one of Johnnie's good friends. Both of their husbands were history professors and they all belonged to the same country club. The Stevens's children had completed high school, their girl went into the Service, the Navy, and was making a good career; their boy was a student at Pasadena City College, PCC.

Another neighbor, Paul Critchen, showed up right after Stan and Barb. He was divorced, and with the help of Lionel, he had custody of his two boys full time. He was attending the dinner to see about making some money for retirement.

Patrick and Lionel's golfing buddies were next. Tom and Lisa Johnston led and George and Carol Hampton followed. Tom Johnston was a doctor, an obstetrician. Lisa was a stay-at-home mom taking care of their five children, the youngest being two years old. George Hampton ran a successful consulting business, and his wife, Carol, a former high school teacher, now stayed at home with their triplets.

As Johnnie was greeting the last of the guests, she felt a hand on her back. She turned and faced Lionel.

"Lionel, everyone has been asking for you and Linda. I told them Linda was out of town. Was that all right?" Johnnie said as she moved quickly away from her host, hoping it wasn't obvious.

"That's fine and thanks for helping out. Now let's join the others," Lionel said moving close once again.

They joined the others who were having a very good time. Lionel always provided the best of everything, including liquor and fine wines. As Johnnie walked into the solarium, she could feel Lionel's hand once again on her back.

Not finding Patrick right away, she hurried over to a group listening to Dr. Tom's baby delivery stories. Somehow, the stories were funny even though she remembered the pain of giving birth three times; everyone was laughing and having a good time including Johnnie. She hid a squeak in her laughter when someone pinched her rear. Her smile froze and she whirled around, but there was no man or woman close enough to accuse at the point. The perpetrator had moved quickly. Johnnie searched the crowd and found Patrick. She whispered that someone had pinched her. He couldn't hear over the High Notes and the noise of the crowd, so she had to repeat several times until she was hissing.

"Here, stand in front of me and I'll guard your rear," Patrick offered, pulling Johnnie in front of him once he finally understood what she was saying.

Johnnie really wanted to go home because the evening was just too bizarre. But she stayed and they all had a wonderful dinner. They sat at the table with their friends Stan and Barb, and Patrick's golfing buddies Tom and Lisa, and George and Carol.

"Lionel really knows how to do a great dinner. The Chablis Cru with the first course, that delicious salmon dish, was superb. And the Cabernet Sauvignon served with the beef was beyond words; it was fine music, not like our High Notes," Stan said, sighing after finishing the delicious meal.

"I see Lionel is serving French wines this evening. I've heard whispers that some of the California wineries may have the start of a very serious problem with phylloxera," George added helpfully, always liking to give the pompous Stan the business whenever he could.

"I hadn't heard that, George. If that's true, it's very serious. I'll have to do some checking on it," Stan said seriously.

"What is phylloxera, Stan, and I am saying it correctly?" Tom asked.

"Phylloxera is a grape louse that is one of the grapevine's worst enemies. It attacks the roots and kills the vine. The French had a terrible problem with this louse in the 1870s and almost lost their entire wine industry."

"So, what did they do about the problem? I know they must have solved it as they are still producing wine," Patrick said.

"They had to get roots from America because at that time American vines were resistant to phylloxera. All of the European vines were pulled up and grafted onto the American vines once the resistance to the louse was discovered. And just a side note, it happens that Chile got their vines from France in the 1860s before the infestation and are phylloxera free," Stan said, answering in full Patrick's inquiry.

Once they'd enjoyed dessert, the crowd was ushered into the large living room with the low sofas. There were plenty of seats for everyone including the High Notes, who'd left their instruments in the solarium so they could listen. Neal Smythe sat next to Johnnie and whispered that they had been given dinner also, and wasn't it wonderful.

Lionel asked the crowd to be quiet so that Charles could give his presentation; then gave a brief introduction of Charles, finishing by stating that he would be discussing a great opportunity for a very good investment.

With that, Charles launched into his briefing, which sounded very good. His financial plan required a $25,000 minimum investment for which they would get quarterly dividends of twenty-plus percent. His plan was believable and he had numbers to back it up. He spoke eloquently about his idea. Almost everyone, including Patrick and Johnnie, couldn't wait to sign up. With everyone busily filling out paperwork, Stan and Barb left quietly.

"Boy, that was a strange evening!" Johnnie whispered to Patrick as they walked home, having finally gotten away from the party. They were the last ones out, leaving Lionel and Charles at the door. Even the High Notes had packed up and left.

"Yes, it truly was different," Patrick said.

Back in their own home they spent no more time discussing the party but instead had a wonderful evening of their own.

Three

The next morning, Johnnie stood in the kitchen preparing breakfast. She was dressed in a pale beige pantsuit with a baby blue print ruffled blouse. Her blonde hair was freshly washed and hanging in waves around her shoulders.

"Thank you for last night, Mrs. Collins," Patrick said coming up from behind Johnnie, hugging her and kissing her softly on her neck.

"And thank you, Mr. Collins," Johnnie said turning around so she could kiss Patrick squarely on the mouth. "Oh, I do love you so, Patrick."

"And I love you." Patrick said.

"Enough of this love stuff, you've got to eat breakfast and get going or you'll be late for your first class." Johnnie said smiling, as she pulled away to finish fixing a simple breakfast.

"I sure don't want much after that big dinner at Lionel's. Don't forget to move the money over to cover the check we wrote last night. Use the money from our 'just-in-case' account, there should be more than enough to cover a check in that amount." Patrick said.

The Collins ate a simple breakfast of cereal, bananas, dry toast, and some more of the Kona coffee as a treat. They ate quietly in the sunny breakfast room that Johnnie had decorated in blue and white with a little yellow. After breakfast, Patrick hurried off, but not before giving his beautiful wife one more kiss.

Johnnie started to clean up the breakfast things when the doorbell rang.

There stood Barb, her dark brown, almost black, hair in short curls around her slightly flushed pale face, her very blue eyes sparkling as she gushed, "Hi, Johnnie."

"Oh, hi, Barb!" Johnnie said enthusiastically. "What brings you out so early this morning?"

"I just want to discuss something with you if it's all right. I saw Patrick leave so I came over," Barb said hesitantly.

"Come on in, I still have some hot coffee since I haven't finished cleaning yet." Johnnie opened the heavy front door wide so her friend could enter.

"So, what did you think of Lionel's meeting last night?" Barb asked once they were seated in the breakfast room with their coffee.

"I thought the dinner was spectacular as always, the speaker was compelling, we even signed up with him. And I was pinched during the cocktail hour," Johnnie said dramatically.

"What! Pinched?! Oh, Johnnie, do you know who did such a thing? I can't imagine who in that group would pinch. I hope you don't think Stan did it. Where were you standing when it happened?" Barb said.

"I was listening to one of Dr. Tom's hilarious baby stories when it happened. I couldn't get turned around fast enough to catch the perpetrator. I do have a couple of suspects though, Lionel Marshall or Bill Carmichael. They were both nearby when I turned around but they had their backs to me. So, they are probably innocent," Johnnie said.

"Oh, Johnnie, I'm sorry that happened. I sure didn't have any indication that any thing like that had happened to you," Barb said.

"I'm glad to hear that, I wouldn't want to give whoever it was the satisfaction of knowing that he got me. By the way, I have to go out this morning and transfer some money to cover the check we wrote last night," Johnnie said.

"If you're going out, then maybe you could help me with something?" Barb said tentatively. "I want to see Charles again so maybe we could go to his office. It's in Pasadena on Lake Street, not too far from Bullock's according to the address on his card."

"You know, I'd like to see Charles again, too. I was a little fuzzy from all the wine last night and there are a few points I would like to have cleared up. If you don't mind coming with me while I do my banking business you can tag along. It will be fun having you. Are you little sweet on Charles, Barb?"

"Oh, I just want to see him one more time. He was so cute and had such a way with words. You know how Stan can be so pompous sometimes but I truly do love him. I just want to see Charles again," Barb said blushing.

"By the way, where was Linda last night," Barb said after she recovered herself.

"I don't know. Lionel was a little vague about where Mrs. Marshall was. He said something about her being out of town to take care of some business. The thing that puzzles me is that I saw Linda a few days ago and we made plans to get together to do some work on decorating my house. She never mentioned she would be going out of town."

"Well, I wouldn't be surprised if the great Mr. Marshall has her buried in the backyard. I really like Linda a lot better than Lionel." Johnnie and Barb laughed for a few more minutes, still tired and a little hung over from the previous evening. Johnnie got up and cleared the table and quickly cleaned the last of the breakfast things and wiped down the very clean kitchen.

"Well, let's go before Lionel gets wind that we're on to him," Johnnie said laughing.

Once Johnnie finished her banking, the ladies headed for Charles Defoe's office. They found the address and decided to park in the Bullock's parking lot because the office was close and parking was at a premium in the area. Once inside the building, they struggled a little to find the upstairs office. It was a beautiful suite, with patio chairs and a table set up on the large balcony through a large sliding glass door. Inside the office, Charles had a large, dark, wood desk with a big executive chair. He had two comfortable chairs in front of the desk and a round table with four chairs secluded in one corner. He certainly looked successful.

"I'm so happy to see you, Barb and Johnnie," Charles said smoothly. "How can I help you ladies?" He was dressed in another finely tailored, pin-striped suit with a yellow rose in his lapel and diamond tie tack on his expensive silk tie.

"Oh, I had a few more questions for you, Charles," Barb said as she pulled out a piece of paper from her purse.

Barb asked her questions, never taking her eyes off Charles as she hung on his every word. Johnnie thought she was being a little obvious but Charles didn't seem to notice; he just continued to pour on the charm. He explained that the program was an investment plan; he would make the investments as a fund, and they would be able to get in on some very big deals that they would probably not be able to do alone. He went on to explain that the interest rate should be very good in these economic times. He pointed out that 1980 was ending well so far, and he thought 1981 would be even better.

Barb asked a few more questions; Johnnie thought she was stalling but didn't know how to interrupt. Charles made no move to stop her. Johnnie was getting hungry because it was nearing the lunch hour, and she finally pulled her friend out of the office.

"Barb, I'm starving. Let's grab something to eat in the Bullock's Tea Room since we are parked in their parking lot," she suggested. So, the ladies walked to Bullock's and went upstairs to the Tea Room. Johnnie ordered the seafood salad with a popover and figured she would exercise energetically when she got home. Barb ordered the daily special. They ate and made comments about the various outfits being modeled. Some of the remarks weren't very nice.

"What did you think of the explanation we got today, Johnnie?" Barb asked over coffee.

"Well, was it all you expected? Really, Barb, weren't you a little obvious there?" Johnnie tried to sound pleasant, but she could hear an accusatory tone in her voice. She just hoped that her friend didn't notice it.

"Oh, I just had to see him again and it was wonderful. Stan and I aren't going to invest at this time." Barb sounded stiff, and a little hurt.

Well, I can't take it back, so maybe we should just leave, Johnnie thought. "Shall we go?" she suggested, after they paid the lunch bill.

The ladies found their car and worked their way through the traffic in the parking lot. It was a big parking lot but it was tight. By the time Johnnie dropped Barb off at her house, both ladies were laughing about their visit to see Charles Defoe.

Four

Johnnie decided to drive on into the office and see her Aunt Rose. Johnnie was her favorite relative, as Aunt Rose was childless. She'd been extremely successful in her lifetime, taking the business Uncle Ted started and turning it into a thriving concern after his sudden death. It was therapy for Rose as she always told Johnnie.

The office was in Alhambra off Huntington Drive. Johnnie helped her Aunt in the business office on a regular basis. The manufacturing section was separate and Johnnie didn't go in the building for any reason. She had been in it once, it was very noisy, and the machinery was big and scary.

When she entered, Aunt Rose got up from her desk and came around it to give Johnnie a big hug. Rose was tall and thin with gray hair twisted up into a bun. She always wore very severe business suits and today was no exception. Her only decoration was a lapel pin showing an old fashioned sailboat, the big kind, like Christopher Columbus came over on.

"Johnnie, I wasn't expecting you today after your big party and all. How did it go? You must tell me. Come sit over here and we'll have Sarah bring in some coffee," Aunt Rose declared as she led Johnnie over to her conference table.

Johnnie explained what the investment was as much as she understood it. She told her aunt that they had invested in it as had most of the people at the party. Her aunt listened carefully and asked a few questions while they drank their coffee.

"Johnnie, it sounds all right. What with the big interest rates that are promised by some economists it shouldn't be too risky. And you didn't put in too much so you should be okay. I think things will be

26

looking up now that we'll probably have Reagan for our President."

"Oh, I'm not going to vote for him so I hope everything will go okay," Johnnie laughed. She knew that her Aunt Rose was a staunch Reagan supporter.

"Did I hear Reagan talk in here?" a male voice teased.

"Is that you, Scott?"

At that point, Scott was far enough in the room that the ladies could see that it was indeed Johnnie's son. He was carrying some papers for Aunt Rose to read and sign. Leaving the papers on her desk, he strolled over to the conference table and stood behind his mom.

"Mom, I didn't think you'd be in today after going to Lionel and Linda's last night. How did that go?" Scott inquired, rubbing his mother's shoulders.

"It went fine. Your father and I decided to invest and hope that we do all right. The numbers looked good. By the way, Linda wasn't there. Lionel said she had gone out of town to do some business or something. He really was sort of vague about it," Johnnie answered.

"Oh, Mother, Linda is probably out of town just like he said. He was most likely just distracted by the party. You know that Lionel is very uptight and a true type A if ever I saw one," Scott said.

"Why don't you join us for a minute, Scott, and we can have a quick little meeting. There's some things I want to go over about the business with you two," Aunt Rose said, motioning Scott to a seat next to her.

Scott sat down and waited to hear what was on her mind. He was a little apprehensive because Aunt Rose had been distracted lately.

"Scott and Johnnie, I have decided to take a lesser role in the company and sort of work up to being retired. I didn't think I would ever say such a thing, thought I would be carried out of here feet first.

"No, don't look so sad. There are some good opportunities for the business right now. Our customers are starting to get more business and that means we, as subcontractors, will have some good opportunities. Scott, you've had lots of experience in this company working here summers since high school and now a couple of years full time since college. I'll work with you for a while but then I would like to travel, see some of the world. I know you probably weren't expecting this but it had to happen some day." Rose finished her speech, took a deep breath, and waited for their reaction.

Scott and Johnnie were speechless for a few minutes.

"Aunt Rose, I would be honored to have such a responsibility," Scott managed to stammer.

"This is all just so sudden, Aunt Rose," Johnnie choked out. "I know Scott will do his best for your company and I will do what I can to help him. So, you want to see the world, do know where you will go first?"

"I'm just not sure where I want to go, London, or Paris, or maybe New York. I just don't know exactly where I'll start. I'd like to see the Grand Canyon up close, maybe by mule. I don't know, just lots of places I've never seen personally," Rose said dreamily.

"Well you certainly have earned a rest but we'll miss you terribly. Your effort made this company what it is today. But will you really be happy away from the company?" Scott said.

"I'm worried about that too. So I'm going to take a month's vacation after the holidays just to see if I can survive without coming in each day." With that said, Rose stood and walked toward her desk, ending the meeting and discussion.

Johnnie and Scott got up also and walked silently out of the office. Johnnie didn't stop to talk with her son; she was just too upset and confused by Aunt Rose's announcement. She drove home pensively, wondering how she would break the news to Patrick. He would definitely worry about the time commitment she'd need to make to help out. Johnnie hadn't counted on giving more time to the business than she already was; she really didn't have too much more to offer. Besides, she didn't have an MBA like Scott, only a BS in mathematics.

To settle her thoughts, Johnnie decided to concentrate on pleasing her husband. Cooking was a favorite pastime, so she began fixing one of Patrick's favorite snacks, a shrimp toast recipe that she got from a Chinese cooking class she took a couple years ago. The recipe was a bit fussy but that didn't bother Johnnie, as she was no longer tired. In fact, she was charged up. As she chopped the ingredients, she wondered just how to phrase the news so that Patrick wouldn't panic and close out what she was saying. The problem was that Johnnie herself felt panic. She decided to make a stir-fry with lots of vegetables and chicken chunks and some rice to go along with the shrimp toast. She would make a dessert of mandarin oranges and some other ingredients.

Johnnie heard Patrick's car through the open kitchen window. She checked her appearance in the mirror on the inside of the broom closet. She had changed into a long flowing outfit that billowed when she walked. Her hair was pulled back from her face in a ponytail; she tucked a loose strand behind her ear. She walked to the door where Patrick would be coming in, unlocked and opened it. Then she stood holding the door in her most alluring way hoping to soften him up.

When he got out of the car carrying a bulging leather briefcase, the one he brought student papers home in, her heart sank. Patrick was always very distracted when he brought papers home, almost impossible to talk to. Johnnie took a deep breath and said, "Hello, sweetheart, I see you have your work cut out for you tonight. Don't worry I have a quick dinner planned."

"Oh, Johnnie, that's great. I really have a lot of work to do this evening. I don't know why I do this to myself sometimes," Patrick sighed.

They walked into their house side by side, Patrick a little dejected and Johnnie apprehensive.

"Do you have time for a quick cocktail and some shrimp toast before you start grading all those papers?"

"That sounds really good, but could you make it wine as I should really concentrate when I'm reading them?" Patrick answered his wife in relief.

Johnnie got busy in the kitchen, finishing the last steps of the shrimp toast. She chose a bottle of already chilled California Chardonnay for their wine. She arranged the hot toast on a nice serving tray, then added the wine along with a bottle opener, two glasses, and plates along with some napkins. She took a deep breath, put a nice smile on her face, and walked with the tray to their living room where Patrick was waiting after dropping his briefcase in his study.

He rose from his comfortable chair and took the tray from his beautiful wife, setting it down on the buffet level chest placed at one corner of the room. The ornate chest had belonged to Johnnie's grandmother and the chest had been a housewarming present from her mother when they moved into their present home. Patrick took a swig of the wine and swirled it around in the glass. Then he sniffed the wine, took a swallow and swished it around in his mouth all with great drama.

"Are you making fun of Stan?"

"Fine bodied wine, will go good with shrimp and chicken," Patrick intoned.

Johnnie laughed again. It was good to see her husband having some fun and relaxing. It gave her courage to launch into Aunt Rose's retirement.

"Patrick, Scott and I got some news from Aunt Rose that really surprised us today…in fact, it left us speechless for a while. She is actually planning to be semi-retired, traveling and seeing the world right after the holidays," Johnnie spilled out quickly.

"That is a big surprise. I never expected the old gal to leave the place she loves so. What did Scott think of all this?"

"We didn't get much time to talk and I really didn't want to. I need to think about this for a while; it's just all so sudden. I know Scott has experience in the company, but he is only twenty-six and doesn't have as many of life's experiences as he may need," Johnnie said.

"Honey, I can't really believe that Aunt Rose will retire completely. I have a feeling that she'll just cut down some of the time she spends there. You know she spends hours upon hours at that company. I just hope you won't have to spend a lot more hours there," Patrick said thoughtfully.

The couple was sitting side by side on their lovely but comfortable sofa, staring out the bay window, watching the sky grow darker as the sun set. They ate their shrimp toast slowly, letting it get cold as the time went on, and just sipped their wine. Their appetites were dying as they talked. Johnnie finally got up and finished the rest of the dinner, which they ate along with the rest of the wine. With a kiss for his wife, Patrick retired to his study with his student papers. Johnnie cleaned up the kitchen and then went to the exercise room at the back of the house on the first floor to work off her steam.

Johnnie changed from the billowy thing to her workout outfit of leotard and tights. She carefully hung her good outfit on a hanger in the closet. The home gym was in a downstairs bedroom that they had converted when they moved in. They used this room when they didn't care to go the gym at their country club. There was special music there for Johnnie to work out with, a treadmill, and Ian's Solo Flex machine.

Her favorite piece of equipment, though, was a bar on one wall with a mirror behind it like a ballerina would use. Johnnie was too tall to be a ballerina but had studied dance as a child and liked to keep up the exercises. After changing, she started with warm-up exercises on the bar, then worked out on the treadmill for a half hour, switched to do a little weight training routine on the Solo Flex machine that Ian had shown her to help with her swimming, followed by some more bar exercises. By the time she was through, she felt much better even though she was breathing hard, and decided to take a bubble bath.

Taking her outfit off the hanger and carrying it with her, she used the back stairs in the kitchen to go up to her bedroom. She stopped again to look at the pictures of her children, taking an extra moment at the picture of Scott and sighing. When she finished her bubble bath, she felt so much more positive. Patrick was right; Aunt Rose probably wouldn't really retire altogether. She had no real hobbies…and how much would she really like traveling since she never made any trips before? *Yes, Patrick is probably right,* she thought as she drifted off to a deep sleep not even being aware of Patrick when he slipped into bed very late that night.

November

We must not inquire too curiously into motives...

Middlemarch, G. Elliot, 1871

Five

Johnnie sighed as she considered her recipes and grocery list for the next couple of weeks in her own little office. Thanksgiving was the next Thursday, which meant both Ian and Colleen would be home along with her mother from Santa Barbara. Aunt Rose would host Thanksgiving dinner as always, but she needed to plan for the other days. There would certainly be a full house for a while. She was happy to have everyone coming but she was tired this Friday afternoon. Work at Aunt Rose's had been heavy the last couple of weeks; Scott was trying to learn the business from Aunt Rose and they were getting lots of orders. Johnnie looked forward to having a holiday weekend and not having to think about the business.

She did her planning in a small bedroom at the end of the kitchen, probably the cook's room in a different time, which had been converted into a home office. She had shelves for her recipe books, a nice desk, a typewriter, and a file cabinet. Patrick kept his wine cellar on the northern wall. He didn't have a big collection but it was a good representation of some of California's finest cabernet sauvignon, Chardonnay, pinot noir, and zinfandel.

Maybe the wines aren't as pricey as Lionel's, but they're very good wines that we can serve with pride, Johnnie thought as she stared at that wall. Tonight, almost one month after the first meeting, they would once again be going to a party at Lionel's, a cocktail party, to hear another briefing from Charles Defoe. *Were they foolish to want to hear him again?* Aunt Rose always said not to risk more than you could afford to lose. Another $25,000 would just about be all they could comfortably afford to throw away. But they really shouldn't worry about losing their money, what with the economy rising just like Charles Defoe had predicted.

Getting up from her desk, she walked out of the office, through the kitchen, and out into the hall, then down the hall past the foyer, the living room and, turning to the front of the house, she knocked on Patrick's study door.

"Honey, we better start getting ready for Lionel's cocktail party. Remember he wants us there early again to help with the guests, etc. At least he asked this time," Johnnie called as she knocked.

"Come on in, sweetie," Patrick answered.

Johnnie stepped into Patrick's very masculine study and admired again the leather chairs and settee, the large dark wood desk, the old-fashioned file cabinets, shelves, and dark paneling. The only jarring note was a desk lamp, purely utilitarian, used to focus some light on his work in the dark room. The desk was piled with student's papers and Patrick looked tired.

"Are you going to be up to the party this evening?" Johnnie said, seeing how tired Patrick looked.

"Lionel is counting on us, we can't miss it," Patrick replied. "Besides, I really want to see about putting some more money in. We got such a good letter from Charles saying how the economy is rising, and that he's made some great investments, promising a dividend at the end of December that will really please all of us. Besides, it will be good to get away from the papers for a while, although I do hope to have them done before the holiday. No sense in the students getting a good holiday and me working. Some how I didn't plan this right."

Patrick and Johnnie walked arm in arm back down the hall to the beautiful front staircase and walked up it to their bedroom. Patrick went off to use the bathroom down the hall now that the kids weren't home so that both he and Johnnie could take showers. They needed to hurry because time had gotten away from them.

Johnnie took a quick shower, washing her hair. Getting out of the shower, while she was drying her hair, she thought about the last gathering at Lionel's and hoped the partygoers would be better behaved. But just in case, she chose a cocktail dress with a full, flowing skirt. It was grayed navy blue chiffon over a satin under-dress, with a fitted bodice and some chiffon coming up over the shoulders. Johnnie didn't like to wear strapless gowns. She added some of her best gold jewelry with diamond accents, a necklace and dangling earrings. She dressed her freshly cleaned hair in an upsweep and fastened it with a sparkling clip. Knowing they would probably walk again, she chose a pair of low-heeled fancy sandals even though she would have preferred some very high heels. Johnnie checked her appearance in the full-length mirror. The dress showed more of her curves than she probably wanted, but the full skirt would help to prevent any more pinching.

"Wow! You'll be the best dressed woman, with the greatest figure, the most beautiful gal at the party," Patrick exclaimed, whistling as he wrapped his arms around his wife, being careful not to spoil any part of her outfit.

"Oh, Patrick, what am I going to do with you?" Johnnie teased, kissing him passionately.

"Do you really want to go to the party or should we stay home and have our own party?"

"If we did, Lionel would be on the phone to start with, then pounding on the door if we didn't answer. Then he would probably call 911 and tell them he thought we were dead. Otherwise, I sure would love to stay here with you," Johnnie told him as she played with Patrick's tie. "I'm going to have to keep my eye on you because you are going to be the most handsome man at the party in that black suit I just love on you."

"Okay, let's go then," Patrick said resigning himself to the party. "Better take a wrap; it's cold out there and we will be walking again since his house is so close by."

Patrick helped Johnnie with her very lovely faux fur silver fox cape that ended at the waist. With that, the couple took off for Lionel's house, walking briskly because it was cold and dampish outside and probably in the high forties. They were slightly breathless when they rang Lionel's doorbell.

Six

This is certainly different from the last party, when Lionel opened the door before we could hardly knock on it. Wonder where he is? We didn't mix up the time did we?" Johnnie spoke softly just in case Lionel was on the other side of the door.

"Let's ring one more time then get out of here," Patrick whispered.

At that moment the door opened and there stood Lionel, not quit finished dressing.

"Oh dear, did we get the time wrong?"

"No, I'm just behind. I really need your help with the caterers this evening if you could," Lionel said distractedly.

"I guess Johnnie would know more about that sort of thing than me, so it's up to her," Patrick said.

"I don't mind. Is Linda away still?" Johnnie said as casually as she could.

"She's not here this evening," was the only reply she got.

After the greeting, Lionel took them into his house and deposited Johnnie with the caterers after taking her wrap and purse. Johnnie hoped Patrick was paying attention to where Lionel put the wrap and purse in case they needed to leave in a hurry. Their host was starting to give Johnnie the willies.

"Oh, miss, what do you want us to do with these meatballs?"

Johnnie stopped to stare at the caterer in confusion. "Don't you have chafing dishes?"

"We're already using them for other hot dishes. Mr. Marshall said he would provide a dish for these meatballs that he especially requested," the caterer explained.

"Well, let me look. I think I know where to find a big chafing dish in Mrs. Marshall's kitchen," Johnnie said rummaging through the cupboards. "Here it is, I knew I could find it."

"Okay, miss. Thanks."

Johnnie was kept running trying to find things that Linda could have easily given to the caterers, coffee containers, extra plates and dishes, and even an ice bucket. After her experience with the caterers, she was looking forward to a nice glass of wine and made the bar her first stop on her way out of the kitchen.

"Oh, hello, Charles!" Johnnie said holding on to her wine glass, trying not to spill all over him. "I didn't hear you come up behind me."

"I didn't mean to startle you, Mrs. Collins, I mean Johnnie," Charles said as he helped steady the glass. "You look lovely this evening."

"Thank you, Charles. Have you seen Patrick? I'm looking for him." Johnnie said.

"Yes, he's in the front with Lionel greeting the guests," Charles said.

"Don't you want to be there, too?" Johnnie asked.

"Yes, let's both go," Charles said resting his hand on Johnnie's bare back.

She didn't know what to do; she certainly did not want his hand on her back but she couldn't move very fast with the wine in her hand. She was beginning to regret getting the wine now; this evening was going to be too stressful to get tipsy. She found a nearby table while they walked and carefully set the glass down. The waiters would have to find it. Then, she moved away from the hand on her back.

They joined Lionel and Patrick, sitting in the foyer on a small sofa. There were a couple of other chairs that Charles and Johnnie sat in before Lionel or Patrick, deep in conversation, noticed that they had entered the room. The doorbell rang, bringing all of them to their feet.

After Johnnie admitted the first guests, she walked them into the solarium. The plan was for Lionel to continue answering the door, while Patrick and Johnnie got the guests settled with drinks and appetizers. It seemed a little awkward, as these people were strangers to the Collinses; they were people that Lionel knew professionally.

Johnnie began regretting her choice of dress early in the evening. All the men were ogling her and some were making what she considered fresh comments. Some of the women were looking at her with evil eyes. She just smiled and made small talk with all of them and wished she hadn't dumped the glass of wine. Now she was thinking she would get a cocktail instead as this evening was worse than the first dinner meeting, because not only was it strange but she didn't know anyone. It wasn't that she was shy, but she was quiet and found it hard meeting new people. She didn't like to be the center of attention, and the blasted dress was certainly making her one.

"Oh, miss, can you come out to the kitchen for a minute," one of the waiters quietly said to Johnnie.

"Oh, okay," Johnnie said, sighing. *Now what?*

In the kitchen, Johnnie found herself in the middle of on an intense argument. She resentfully wondered where Lionel was. If Linda had been here this would have been her problem.

"He wants to bring the Brie out after everyone is here and really it needs to be out when they arrive. We have a hot tray to keep it warm," the head caterer said.

"It just won't be as good warmed as it would be fresh from the oven. Can't you understand that? I'm the chef, I know what I'm doing. The pastry just won't hold up that well," the man in the white hat said.

The argument was at full pitch and very intense. Johnnie just didn't want to deal with it so she excused herself and went to find Lionel. *It's his party, he should be taking care of things,* she thought to herself bitterly.

"Lionel, I've been looking for you. There's a problem in the kitchen that you need to settle before there is a fist fight."

"Johnnie, I need you to keep peace in the kitchen, just do what you need to do!" Lionel barked.

Johnnie, livid, was taken aback. She marched back to the kitchen, her full skirt flowing wildly.

"All right, if the chef wants the Brie brought out after the guests are all here then get one of the waiters to help," Johnnie said with a firmness and look that could not be argued with. Being 5'8" in her bare feet, and with her very good posture, Johnnie made a commanding presence when she needed to.

After leaving the kitchen, she hoped for the last time, she headed for the bar. It was crowded there and so she waited in line and made small talk with the people around her. As she waited, she heard a low sinister voice in her ear,

"You are so beautiful."

Johnnie whirled around but there was no one there. Was she hallucinating? She felt a chill go down her spine and shivered.

"Are you cold?" One of Lionel's business partners looked at her in concern.

"No, I'm okay," Johnnie replied with one of her biggest smiles.

"Tell me what you'd like to drink this evening, and I'll get it for you. By the way, we didn't formally meet yet. My name is Hal Brisbee."

"I'm Johnnie Collins, one of Lionel's neighbors, and I'll have a Tom Collins, please," Johnnie said and hoped it would be strong.

"Well, Mrs. Collins, having a little of your husband," Hal said joking and leering.

"What? Oh no, my husband is Patrick not Tom," Johnnie said, deliberately missing his joke.

Once she had her drink, she headed for the hors d'oeuvres thinking this evening would never end. She walked around the table, studying the choices carefully as she sipped her cocktail and thought about the tasteless joke she had endured.

"Try the shrimp with the sauce, it's very good. And do get some of the Brie, they just brought it out and it's exquisite. These little meatballs are especially good, surprisingly enough. By the way, I'm Paul Graham, a colleague of Lionel's," said the man standing next to her, as he loaded up his plate.

Paul was a short dumpy man in a rumpled suit, balding, but with a fringe of light brown curly hair. He seemed pleasant and harmless enough, so Johnnie introduced herself, then joined him at the end of the solarium where little tables had been placed for the evening. A man was playing a guitar softly and singing in a low voice, folk songs, old ones from the sixties if Johnnie was hearing correctly. *How very odd,* she thought.

"Johnnie, there you are!"

"Have you been looking for me, Patrick?"

"Just all over, that's all," her husband replied with a smile.

Johnnie introduced her companion as Patrick sat down at the table with them.

"Have you tried any of the hors d'oeuvres? They are excellent, Lionel really knows how to do a first class party," Paul made small talk with Patrick.

"I've had a few nibbles and everything was very good. Lionel does like his entertainment first rate," Patrick said squeezing Johnnie's arm.

Johnnie stayed at the table for a while listening to the old folk songs. The singer sang "All My Sorrows," "Where Have All the Flowers Gone?" and others Johnnie couldn't remember the titles of but recognized the words and sang them to herself. Patrick left at one point and freshened her drink. Paul left at another point and brought back a couple of plates of food for them to share.

"Lionel wants us to stay for dinner after the others have left," Patrick told Johnnie while Paul was gone.

"Oh, do you really want to?" Johnnie said in a sort of whine after all the strong cocktails she'd finished.

"I can't think of a reason why we can't, no babies at home, no dog waiting for dinner, no previous engagement. If you can think of something we'll get out of it."

"How about sick and tired of Lionel?" Johnnie leaned over and whispered to Patrick.

"That would do it all right," Patrick said laughing. "Oh, that looks good Paul, let me help you."

"I tried to get some of everything. It was starting to get crowded around the table. Guess people are getting hungry. Do you know why we are here tonight? Lionel mentioned something about money," Paul said.

"Yes, Charles Defoe will be giving a presentation on a interesting proposal. Johnnie and I already joined up with the plan at the last party Lionel gave, and we plan to add some more money this evening. The economy is really taking off at the end of 1980 after starting out so bad."

"Ah yes, the economic sanctions against Russia, then no Olympics. Then there was that tragic attempt to rescue the hostages in Iran, so, so sad, and then Mt. St. Helens. Who'd have thought it would erupt so spectacularly, certainly not Harry Truman, the man, not the President. Now we've got Reagan, a movie star for our next President," Paul said as he filled his plate.

Lionel came into the room ringing a little bell at that moment.

"Boys and girls, could you please come with me to the foyer where we will hear an informative discourse from our honored guest, Mr. Charles Defoe," Lionel sang out.

There were some groans as the guests rose from wherever they had settled and walked with Lionel to the foyer. Walking in the crowd, Johnnie felt somewhat crushed, even holding Patrick's hand. In her ear, she heard the same sinister voice as before,

"You are so beautiful."

Johnnie shuddered as a chill crept down her spine and quickly squeezed Patrick's hand.

"Everything all right, Johnnie? Are you cold?"

"I'm not cold, just disgusted. Remind me to tell you about it later."

Lionel had chairs set up in the foyer, but no tables, so it was awkward for those who brought drinks and plates. Charles, dressed in a beautifully tailored dark suit with the same diamond tie tack, was even more compelling this evening. He began by saying that the early investors could count on a great dividend at the end of December, and if the economy went the way people were predicting, then even greater dividends would be given in 1981. He had all sorts of charts and numbers to back up his theory. He got an enthusiastic response from his audience and many signed up with him, including Patrick and Johnnie once again.

It was just about ten p.m. when the last of the guests left. Then Johnnie, Patrick, Charles, Lionel, and an unknown woman were seated at a table that was brought into the foyer after the chairs were cleared. The woman was not as tall as Johnnie, probably 5'5", in a very form-fitting black, strapless cocktail dress painted over her full figure. She had thick, black hair piled on top of her head, with flashy earrings and a diamond pendant necklace. She wore very high heels that made her Johnnie's height, as Johnnie wore her low heels. Johnnie wondered if this other woman suffered as many leering stares as she had had to endure.

The dinner started with clear soup, then continued with a small first course of a pasta dish with tomatoes and cream; the main course was roasted duck, with Lyonnaise potatoes, and a vegetable casserole. The final course was a salad of romaine lettuce, grapefruit and orange sections, and pomegranate seeds, in a deliciously light dressing of olive oil and orange juice. The dinner ended with coffee. Johnnie didn't pay much attention to anyone in particular as she was tired and really just wanted to go home. She picked at her food even though it was excellent and tried to keep a pleasant look on her face. She even avoided the wines because she knew she still had to walk home and really had had enough to drink. She noticed Patrick also was going easy on the wine and was grateful.

Seven

The next morning, Johnnie slept late, she treated herself and didn't roll out of bed until eight-thirty a.m. Patrick was long gone, off on the golf course with Lionel and the rest of his foursome. Stretching as she crossed to the bathroom, she thought about her unpleasant evening. The food was excellent, beyond compare, really, the house was clean and fresh, the entertainment strange but good, so what really was wrong with the party? The guests and the host. *Who had talked in her ear in that creepy way?* When she thought back on the two incidents, she remembered seeing Lionel in both scenes, maybe not close enough, but he was there.

After showering, she dressed in jeans, a sweater, and sensible shoes and hurried down to the kitchen to get coffee and a quick breakfast because her cleaning crew was coming for the morning. She wanted the house nice and clean when her daughter and mother arrived on Tuesday. The plan was for Colleen to pick up her grandmother on the way down from Palo Alto, a little out of her way but doable.

While she was waiting for the toast, she put some well-used cards into her recipe box and thought about Linda. *Where is she? Is she divorcing Lionel? Could that be why he was so cross last night?* When the toast was nice and brown, she ate quickly knowing the maids would be there any minute. In fact, she just took her last swallow of coffee when there was a knock on her kitchen door.

"Hello, Mrs. Collins, we're here to work."

"Come on in, ladies, and we'll get started."

The ladies, six of them in various ages and sizes, marched in with all the equipment needed to make the house sparkle...not that it didn't already. The head lady, Pearl, made the assignments, then the ladies all took off to their various rooms. Blanca was to work in the kitchen with Mrs. Collins. She and Johnnie worked for a while with Blanca sniffing the entire time.

"Are you getting a cold, Blanca?" Johnnie felt bad for her, but still wished Blanca had stayed home if that was the case.

"No, I don't have a cold," Blanca said.

Johnnie suddenly realized that her helper was holding back tears. *Now what,* Johnnie sighed to herself. She really wasn't up to much this morning, not after all the rich food and drink the night before.

"Oh, Mrs. Collins, I just don't know what Henry and I are going to do. We have to move out of the place we are living in and can't find any place we can afford. We have to be out by December first. I just don't know what we're going to do. I don't want to be in a hotel or out on the streets. I'm just so worried," Blanca said trying not to cry.

Johnnie was worried because Blanca was one of her best maids and her husband, Henry, was their gardener.

"Well, let me think for a minute. There's the chauffeur's quarters above the garage. It has a couple of rooms, a sort-of kitchen, and a bathroom. It probably needs a little work and I know the stairs need fixing. I'll have to talk with my husband but I think it should be all right," Johnnie said thoughtfully.

"Oh, Mrs. Collins, that would be wonderful. Thank you, thank you," Blanca said forgetting herself and hugging Johnnie.

"Well, don't forget I have to talk with Mr. Collins first. He'll be home in a couple of hours."

With that, the women continued to work, making the kitchen shine even more than it had before they started.

After they finished, Johnnie sat at her desk to plan dinner for the evening. She would need to soften up Patrick for this latest adventure. Checking the time, she decided she had enough to go to the club and swim a few laps before dropping by Bristol Farms and picking up the few items she needed for dinner.

She changed into a softer outfit, still casual, but nicer than her cleaning clothes, gathered up her swimsuit and the other paraphernalia she would need, grabbed a jacket because it was cold and threatening rain, and took off after seeing the cleaning crew out. At the country club she walked straight to the pool, not stopping to chitchat with anyone because her time was short. Forty minutes later, she was on her way out when she heard someone call her name.

"Johnnie, oh Johnnie, wait up!"

Turning, Johnnie saw Barb walking very fast and waving her arms. Johnnie wanted to run for her car, but didn't.

"Hi, Barb," Johnnie said without her usual enthusiasm.

"Johnnie, I was hoping to catch you," Barb panted. "Do you have time for a cocktail?"

"Not really, but maybe a quick cup of coffee.

They sat in a booth near the entrance to the little coffee bar of the country club, and Johnnie hoped that the visit wouldn't be long. It was going on two o'clock, and Patrick would be arriving home soon.

"So, what did you want to talk about, Barb?" Johnnie asked.

"The party at Lionel's last night, of course. Was Linda there? Who were the guests? Did you have a nice time?"

"Charles was there and looked great. The party was odd. No, Linda was not there and I had to run the kitchen," Johnnie said.

"You had to run the kitchen? I can't believe Lionel asked you to do that."

"Yes, all in all it was another bizarre evening at the Marshalls'. I can't really give you all the details right now, but maybe Sunday after church when the guys are watching football you and I can have our own little meeting. I really have to run now," Johnnie said as she picked up her swim stuff and prepared to leave.

"Oh that sounds good. Those football games get to me."

With that, the two women went their separate ways; Johnnie drove down to Bristol Farms, and lucked into a great space right in the front of its parking lot on Lake Street. She quickly gathered up the items she needed and drove carefully home. Whenever she felt rushed, she tried to make herself drive extra carefully, believing firmly that time should not be made up on the road.

Eight

Johnnie put the groceries up quickly, and then went upstairs to change her clothes one more time. She put on some soft beige slacks and a pale blue fuzzy sweater. She decided to wear a choker of pearls and pearl drop earrings. Her blond, wavy hair settled gently on her shoulders. She hoped she had the right look, alluring yet vulnerable. She wore just a small dab of Shalimar perfume.

Back in the kitchen, she covered her outfit with an apron and got busy. She was going to have roasted garlic on toasts for the appetizer. They would have their Caesar salad first, and then steak au poivre along with potatoes Dauphinoise with wild mushrooms, and Brussels sprout halves tossed in lemon butter. Dessert would be a fruit tart purchased from Bristol Farms. She roasted the garlic and prepared the small slices of bread to be dried out in the oven. She crushed the peppercorns for the steak. Then she tore up the romaine lettuce for the salad and prepared the dressing to be added to the lettuce at the table. As she finished the salad preparation, she saw Patrick drive up through the kitchen window. Quickly putting on a less utilitarian apron, she hurried across the kitchen and opened the door for her returning husband.

"How did it go today, Patrick?" Johnnie said.

"Not too bad. I shot in the low eighties," Patrick replied, carrying his golf bag in and depositing it in a large closet off the kitchen.

"Dinner will be ready about seven with cocktails at sixish," Johnnie said.

"In that case, I'll change then go to my study for awhile. Call me when it's time for the cocktails." As he passed by, Patrick gave his wife a nice kiss.

50

Johnnie smiled to herself, knowing that Patrick would be stretching out on the sofa in his study for a little siesta before dinner. Changing back into her utilitarian apron, she got busy with the potato dish. She sliced the potatoes in the Cuisinart and rehydrated the dry wild mushrooms. She put together the potatoes Dauphinoise and refrigerated them for the short time before they would need to go in the oven. She prepared the Brussels sprouts, steaming them for a short while so she'd be ready to finish them at the last minute. Next, she removed the garlic from the oven and spread the creamy paste over the toast. She decided on Scotch and water for their evening drink, knowing that Patrick would choose the wine for dinner. She fixed a tray with the hors d'oeuvres; the Scotch and glasses were already in the chest in the living room, so all she needed was the ice bucket, which she filled with ice. Before leaving the kitchen, she popped the potatoes in the oven.

Going down the hall, and then turning to the front of the house, she knocked softly on Patrick's study door.

"Honey, it's cocktail time," Johnnie called sweetly.

"Huh? Oh, okay, I'm coming."

Patrick opened the door and hugged and kissed Johnnie fervently. She kissed him back with equal passion.

"Come on, lover, I've prepared a good dinner for you tonight," Johnnie said, taking his hand and leading him to the living room.

Patrick fixed the Scotch and water for them and they sat on the sofa munching the garlic toasts and sipping as they watched the sun set.

"So, what did you do today in my absence?" Patrick teased.

"I had the cleaning crew in today," Johnnie said.

"Yes, the house is sparkling," Patrick observed.

"While they were here, Blanca, who's the wife of Henry our gardener, told me about a situation they are facing. They are about to become homeless. They have to move and can't find anything they can afford. I was wondering if they could use the chauffeur's quarters over the garage. I know the stairs need to be repaired and I'm not sure about the actual quarters," Johnnie said.

"I don't want to lose Henry, so do what you have to do. Let's see if we can't get them full time. Then you wouldn't be alone in the house," Patrick said.

"Both Henry and Blanca are students at PCC so I don't know if they'd be willing, or able to work full time," Johnnie said thoughtfully.

"Well, if not full time, then for us exclusively," Patrick said as he rose to go call Henry and set it up. He returned and gave his wife a big hug and said it was all set. Henry would be by tomorrow to see what needed to be done about the stairs and Blanca would come with him to discuss her position.

With that, they went to the dining room and Johnnie mixed the Caesar salad. After the salad, Johnnie went to the kitchen to finish the dinner, cooking the steak and finishing the Brussels sprouts.

"Oh, we're having Brussels sprouts, one of my very favorites!" Patrick exclaimed as he sipped his wine and kept his wife company as she finished the steak au poivre.

She put the steaks on a warm plate, poured the peppery sauce over the top, and sprinkled them with some finely chopped parsley. She put the Brussels sprout halves in a bowl, poured melted butter and lemon over them, and placed some lemon slices artfully over the sprouts. She pulled the potatoes out of the oven, sprinkled them with some more of the chopped parsley, then brought everything to her beautifully set table. They finished the dinner with coffee and the fruit tart.

"Oh, Mrs. Collins, that was truly a remarkable dinner. Here's a kiss for the cook," Patrick said grabbing his wife and kissing her.

"And thank you, kind sir. I'm so glad you enjoyed it," Johnnie answered hugging her husband.

They both carried their plates and other items from the table to the kitchen. Johnnie began working on the cleanup and Patrick helped her.

"I didn't tell you about our golf game today. We took longer; did you notice?" Patrick asked.

"Yes, in the back of my mind as I was fixing dinner. What

happened anyway?" Johnnie said.

"Lionel. He was late and that woman who was at dinner Friday night drove him to the club. Then he kept excusing himself. We actually had to let two parties play through. I don't know what was wrong with him," Patrick said.

"Did he tell you who that woman was or even her name?" Johnnie asked.

"No, and none of us asked. Lionel wasn't his usually cordial self. By the way, Linda's still not back; George made a big mistake and asked him. Wow, did Lionel get angry!" Patrick said.

"Oh, don't put water in that pan!" Johnnie said taking the heavy iron pan from Patrick, reaching over him so that her body pressed against his and their arms twisted together.

"Let's call it quits here and head upstairs, my sweet," Patrick said hurrying his wife up the beautiful stairs to their bedroom. Once upstairs, he scooped her up and carried her through the last bit of the hallway. They hadn't been as cautious about their loving since they had the house to themselves. In the bedroom, they made love with a passion they hadn't known since they were very young, and Johnnie forgot about Linda, Aunt Rose, and the dirty dishes in the kitchen. All of her cares were buried in the ardor of the moment.

In the early morning when it was still dark, Johnnie rose from her bed as quietly as possible. She didn't want to disturb Patrick, not after having one of the most pleasurable evenings that she could remember. She wanted to lean over and kiss him before she went downstairs, but if she woke him, he would keep her there and she just had to finish the kitchen. As she stepped carefully over the various piles of clothes thrown on the floor in their haste the previous night, she wondered how she could be thinking about the kitchen after her steamy lovemaking. She didn't know, but she was and she had to finish cleaning the last few dishes. Sometimes she just disgusted herself but she was who she was.

As she worked, she thought about Linda. *Where was she? Why hadn't anyone heard from her?* There was another thing bothering Johnnie that she couldn't discuss with anyone for the time being.

Linda was secretly working on a cookbook and had only told Johnnie. Linda never left her recipes, taking them with her in her very large purse whenever she left the house. So why was the recipe box there in the kitchen when Johnnie worked with the caterers? Why would she leave it? If Linda were really planning on divorcing Lionel, she would need to write a book or something to keep going. She surely wouldn't do well financially against Lionel who was legendary in his brutality in divorce agreements. One really needed to have him on one's side; it was a nightmare to come up against him. *So, why were the recipes out in the open for anyone to just take?* That was really bothering Johnnie as she put everything in its place. With the kitchen cleaned to her satisfaction, Johnnie put the problems with Linda to bed as she quietly climbed back in bed next to her husband.

Nine

When they returned from church that morning, Henry and Blanca were already waiting for them.

"Mr. Collins, I've checked the stairs and believe we can repair them rather than replace them," Henry told Patrick once he and Johnnie were back outside after quickly changing their clothes. Johnnie left the two men to go over the stairs and took Blanca inside with her to discuss her position. Blanca would be the housekeeper and take charge of Pearl and her girls. She would help in the kitchen at first, since she was not an accomplished cook but would like to become one. Neither she nor Henry could give more than about twenty-five hours a week; school had to come first. They would be available to help with parties if given enough notice.

"I've sent Henry off to get the supplies we'll need for the stairs," Patrick said as he came into the house. "Will we have lunch before the game? I'm awfully hungry."

"Something quick. Doesn't the game start pretty soon?" Johnnie asked.

"No, not till three," Patrick said.

Johnnie fixed some tuna salad sandwiches with carrot sticks, olives, and some homemade butter pickles. There was some leftover fruit tart for dessert. Then Johnnie started preparing the snacks for the football game with Blanca's help. It felt good to have another woman in the kitchen with her. They were only having Stan and Barb over so they wouldn't need a huge spread, but Johnnie wanted to fix some substantial snacks to go with all the beer. She and Barb would be in the library at their own little gathering and would be having cocktails, martinis, Barb's favorite drink. Johnnie wanted to be sure to have solid food with the cocktails and not just peanuts.

She and Blanca prepared some stuffed eggs, some little finger sandwiches for the ladies, some bigger sandwiches of roast beef and turkey for the men, guacamole with chips for the guys, and some dill dip with vegetables for the ladies. There were peanuts for both rooms. Then Johnnie and Blanca arranged everything on serving trays and put the trays and drinks on a rolling cart. They deposited the men's snacks and drinks in the sunroom, really the family room but it was very sunny. Then, they rolled the cart to the library where it would stay. Johnnie went up to her bedroom to change into company clothes of apricot cashmere pants with a matching apricot cashmere turtleneck adding a long chunky gold chain, a Christmas gift from Patrick last year. She added chunky gold hoop earrings. Blanca left to join her husband working on the stairs.

The doorbell rang just as Johnnie finished changing. She skipped downstairs, humming a nameless cheery tune, still high from her evening before.

"Hi, Barb and Stan," she sang out as she opened the door.

She immediately noticed and admired her guest's new outfit…Barb wore a gray wool flannel pants suit with a silk print blouse with a bow. She had a pearl swirled pin on the lapel of her jacket and pearl earrings with a touch of diamonds. Stan was dressed not unlike Patrick in a printed sweater, dark slacks, and shoes he could kick off once settled in the family room. They settled in their respective rooms with plenty of time to chat before kick-off. Patrick had built a fire for the ladies in the large fireplace in the library. Everything was warm and cozy as it began to rain again.

"So, let's have a toast to the rain that we always need," Barb said raising her glass.

They tapped their glasses, hers with an olive and Johnnie's with an olive and pickled onion, then each took a large swig. Finishing their first drink a little faster than Johnnie counted on, she poured the next round from the pitcher of martinis that Patrick had mixed for them.

"Let's toast to Thanksgiving," Barb said, raising her glass.

Once again, the ladies touched glasses and this time Johnnie sipped while Barb swigged. Johnnie fixed two plates of appetizers with the hope of slowing things down because she was beginning to feel the two drinks, as Patrick had not been stingy with the liquor. While they were snacking, Johnnie filled Barb in on Patrick's experience at the golf course with Lionel.

"Let's toast Linda, wherever she is," Barb said as she filled both glasses.

Johnnie just took one sip after the ladies tapped glasses. They had been together for over an hour although it seemed like ten minutes to Johnnie.

"Oops, we're dry here, Johnnie," Barb sang out.

"I'll get Patrick to mix some more in a few minutes. He took the fixings in with him and said to call him if we need more. Let's have some more of these snacks, after all, Blanca and I worked hard on these little sandwiches," Johnnie said.

"Do you have a cook?" Barb asked.

"No, a part time housekeeper. Blanca and her husband Henry, our gardener, are moving into our chauffeur quarters. Henry is fixing the steps this afternoon, though I hope not in the rain. I'm going to ask Patrick to have Blanca and Henry stay and cook dinner this evening. It's simple, just a roast in a bag, but I can't do it. Will you and Stan stay for dinner if I can get them to cook it?" Johnnie said.

"We'd love to stay for dinner because I don't think I'd be able to cook tonight either," Barb said.

Johnnie eased herself out of her chair, steadying herself on the arms. Once upright, she moved carefully out of the library down to the family room. Leaning on the door jam, she quietly called to Patrick.

"We're dry in there!" Johnnie whispered.

"Okay, honey, I'll be right down with fresh supplies," Patrick answered softly.

If Patrick noticed that his wife was a little inebriated, he didn't say anything.

"Oh, could you ask Blanca if she could stay and cook dinner this evening. It's a simple meal and I know she can handle it; Henry could help too if he wants," Johnnie said.

"I'll take care of it, sweetie," Patrick said.

Patrick mixed the next batch of martinis and then walked arm in arm with Johnnie back to the library.

"Great, here come the new supplies, we're dry in here," Barb sang out as Johnnie and Patrick walked in carrying the fresh martinis.

Johnnie resumed her seat, flopping back down in the soft cushions. She just played with the olive and onion in her glass and took very small sips when Barb gave toast after toast. They could hear the men yelling and cheering in the family room as the game came to its end. And the men could probably hear the hilarity as it grew louder and louder coming out of the library.

"Johnnie, did that chair swallow you?" Patrick laughed as he came into the room.

Patrick gently helped his wife up out of the chair she had collapsed in. Then the couple moved slowly down the hallway to the dining room, with Barb and Stan slowly following behind. Johnnie ate the dinner Blanca and Henry had prepared with her head in a buzz, trying hard not to spill anything.

"Johnnie, your new help prepared and served such a nice meal. You were lucky to find them and I envy you," Barb said as she cleaned her plate.

"Yes, we feel we are fortunate too," Patrick answered for Johnnie who was just plain dazed.

"The dinner was excellent and the zinfandel was perfect with the pork roast," Stan added. "Hate to eat and run, but I have an early class tomorrow and Barb has to get up early too. Thanks for the fun afternoon and evening and the delicious dinner, you're always such gracious hosts," Stan said as he rose from the table.

"Yes, I'm doing some volunteer work at the school library where I used to teach," Barb said sleepily.

"Oops, I had no idea it was so late, it's almost eleven-thirty," Patrick said checking his watch. "Just wait a minute, I need to take care of something then I'll walk you across the street. Aren't we glad none of us are driving?"

Patrick slipped quickly into the kitchen and returned in a few minutes.

"Johnnie, why don't you wait here and I'll be right back.," Patrick said.

"Bye, Johnnie, it was great fun," Barb said as she stood stretching.

With that, Barb, Stan, and Patrick left Johnnie sitting at the dining room table, smiling and hoping that was what she was supposed to do. It was just a few steps to Stan and Barb's, so Patrick was back in a jiffy to help his wife up the stairs and into bed.

"Honey, you should remember that Barb can drink a lot of men under the table. Just get some sleep, my sweet, and you'll be as good as new tomorrow," Patrick said as he tucked his wife under the covers and pressed a sweet kiss on her forehead.

Johnnie felt quite foolish, but was unable to do much about it. At least Patrick was being kind about her predicament and that made her love him even more. She wanted to reach up and return his kiss but couldn't coordinate the effort so she just kissed the air. Patrick touched her lips very softly and told her again to go to sleep.

Ten

The sun rose long before Johnnie the next morning. Even though it was already eight a.m., she groaned when Patrick brought in his famous "morning after drink." She drank it and gagged.

"Oh, Patrick, did you put raw egg in this?" Johnnie moaned.

"Yes, that's part of the cure," Patrick said cheerily.

"What about salmonella?" Johnnie asked.

"I only used the white part of the egg so it should be okay, besides with lots of hot sauce in it, that should help," Patrick said.

"I trust you and thank you," Johnnie declared as she rose from the bed and gave her husband a big hug with a big kiss.

"Mmm, glad you're feeling better, sweetie," Patrick cooed.

Patrick then left to go to work and Johnnie went to the bathroom to take a good refreshing shower. Once she felt cleaned up, she dressed in a royal blue wool gabardine pantsuit and a white cashmere sweater and added some small gold ball earrings. Her hair fastened at her neck with a tortoise clip. She then walked down to the kitchen to see if by any chance Blanca was there.

"Ah, Blanca, you're here. Thanks again for helping last night; I certainly appreciate it, on such short notice and all. The dinner was really very good so you're a better cook than you think," Johnnie said.

"Thank you, Mrs. Collins, it was our pleasure to help you. Now let me get you some breakfast. Mr. Collins said you were to be sure to have some before you left the house," Blanca said.

"Oh he did, did he? Well bring it on," Johnnie said taking a seat at the table in the breakfast room.

Blanca served Johnnie a healthy breakfast of juice, whole-wheat cereal and banana, with lightly buttered toast, and black coffee. Johnnie ate the breakfast with gusto; surprising herself as she'd thought she wouldn't be able to stomach anything.

"Guess that drink Patrick made me helped after all, even though it was hard to swallow. If the stairs are fixed, let's go look at the quarters to see what needs to be done," Johnnie said.

"Henry is out there now and we can ask him if can use the stairs, Mrs. Collins," Blanca said.

"Oh boy, it's cold out here! The sun fooled me. I thought it would be warm but I guess all the snow on the mountains is making it brisk," Johnnie said as she hugged herself and shivered.

The ladies walked briskly to the garage apartment, which was several car lengths from the house. The newly repaired stairs, smelling like fresh-cut wood, looked very sturdy. Johnnie, Henry, and Blanca walked quickly up the stairs, then waited on the small, cramped landing while Johnnie opened the door with the key she brought. Once they finally got the door opened, they all rushed in. It was dark and cold, the kind of cold a building gets that hasn't had heat for a long time, the kind of cold that goes straight to the bone.

"Oh dear, there's a terrible leftover cigar smell in here," Johnnie said through clattering teeth. "The only way to get rid of this foul odor is to paint the walls, replace the drapes and rugs, and polish the floors. I do hope we can get this work done before you have to move."

"We can start on the cleanup right away since I don't have class till evening today," Henry volunteered.

The three then continued their inventory of the small quarters. There was an adequate living room with an efficiency kitchen on the end close to the small hallway. There was a bar separating the little kitchen from the living room. The two rather small bedrooms were through a door at the end of the dining room.

"These quarters are sort of sweet, if you ignore the smell," Blanca said.

"Yes, I think this apartment will work out quite nicely for you and Henry. We're just so glad to have both of you. I'll see about getting the utilities started and have the gasman out to check the furnace. I think if there are no surprises, you two can move in over Thanksgiving weekend. In the meantime, Blanca, let's you and I go shopping for the new rugs and drapes. We can get the paint after we finish and know what colors we'll want," Johnnie said.

Johnnie and Blanca drove to Colorado Street and found a carpet place that looked promising. After a lot of looking and dickering, which was against Johnnie's nature, the ladies ended up with a floral printed rug for the bedroom, a brown multi-colored carpet remnant for the living room, and a small area rug for the hallway between the kitchen and the two bedrooms and bathroom. Johnnie insisted on pads for all the rugs and made arrangements to have everything delivered.

"Next let's go to Fedco and see what we can find to replace that horrible furniture, that stuff looked a least a hundred years old," Johnnie said as they got into the car.

The ladies were able to find everything that would be needed: bed, drawers, table and chairs, sofa, two easy chairs, and some occasional tables. They also picked out some lamps for the living room and bedroom. Johnnie arranged once again to get everything delivered.

"Well, I can't think of anything else right now that you'll need and I'm pooped. Let's go over to Hutch's and get a bite to eat and rest our feet. How does that sound?" Johnnie asked as she collapsed into the car.

"Oh, that's perfect! Thank you for everything, Mrs. Collins, I know our new home is going to be just beautiful. Thank you, thank you," Blanca gushed.

At Hutch's Johnnie and Blanca both had hamburgers and even though it was November, Johnnie had some of Hutch's delicious ice tea. They were both too full for any of the wonderful deep-dish pie Hutch's had to offer.

"Let's get a hamburger for Henry and head on home. I want to see how things are going and figure out exactly how much paint we'll need," Johnnie said as she was paying the bill.

Johnnie sent Blanca off to Henry with the hamburger and she

went into her own house and to her little office to make some phone calls. She didn't want to just throw out the furniture that was stored in the chauffeur's quarters because it still was usable and would be a shame to waste. She didn't have to make very many calls before she got Good Will to agree to take the furniture. She would get Henry and Ian to move the furniture down to one of the empty garage slots; they had six with two empty slots when everyone was home now that Scott didn't live there. Next, she called an electrician to check the wiring, hoping it wouldn't need replacing because that would be a big job. With everything she could think of done for the moment, she decided to go for a swim at the country club missing Linda more than ever as they swam together almost every day.

Eleven

She heard her name being called as she was leaving the country club after her swim.

"Johnnie, oh, Johnnie, wait up please!"

"Sure, Barb, so we meet again," Johnnie called back.

"Do you have time for a cocktail this time, Johnnie?" Barb asked.

"I can spare a few more minutes, Barb," Johnnie answered.

The ladies seated themselves in a booth in the tastefully appointed bar of the country club and Johnnie ordered a glass of Chardonnay, Barb ordered a Scotch and water. There was a snack mix with peanuts, pretzels, and cereal to munch on.

"I really miss Linda, Barb. You know we used to swim together almost every day. It's just not the same coming here to the club. I have so many swimmers to fight against to get a lane. Linda and I used to really have a lot of fun together. You know how she could really make us laugh. Where is she? I just want to talk with her and see if everything is okay," Johnnie said.

"Johnnie, I know you and Linda were good friends even though we've known each other since college. I really like her too, but let's not talk about her like she's dead for heaven sakes," Barb said.

"I'm just tired, that's all. I believe she will turn up soon and is probably just having a trial separation from Lionel. It's just that she didn't take her recipe box with her and you know, Barb, she didn't go anywhere without it," Johnnie said.

"Okay, Miss Marple, enough already," Barb said, raising her hands in submission. "So how was the party at Lionel's? You were going to tell me something about it yesterday before you got so out of it."

64

"It's hard to explain so that you'll understand and not think I'm nuts," Johnnie said.

"Well, what is it? Tell me quick, inquiring minds want to know!" Barb said.

"Okay. Someone, on two separate occasions, whispered in my ear in the most creepy, slimy way, 'You are so beautiful.' It gave me the creeps in a big way. In fact it reminded me of that old movie from the sixties, *Elvira Madigan*, when she and her amour were getting hard up for money and she had to dance in a bar. An icky man kept bothering her telling her she was beautiful; then when she left the bar, he was waiting for her. I guess all the sixties folk songs made me think of the old movie," Johnnie said.

"Johnnie, that gives me the creeps too. Don't suppose you know who did it? And I remember that old movie. Stan and I couldn't get enough berries with heavy cream. Do you remember that scene when they ate with their hands? Well, of course we didn't eat with our hands, we just ate a lot of berries and cream for a while," Barb said.

"I don't know who said it and they weren't waiting for me outside so I hope I never have to hear it again. Kind of funny not wanting to hear you're beautiful but really I only want to hear that from Patrick," Johnnie said.

"Oh, Johnnie, you are a beautiful woman don't you know that?" Barb said.

"Does anyone ever think they're beautiful? I don't think so. Besides, you're good looking yourself," Johnnie gushed.

"Okay, enough of the mutual admiration society. How is your new help working out?" Barb asked.

"I never thought I would be grateful for help but I sure am. It was great to have my breakfast fixed this morning when I was a little weak. It will be good to have help with all the company coming. I have to make all the beds, etc, and Blanca's help will be appreciated," Johnnie said.

"Do you have time for another?" Barb asked.

"No, I better get home; we need to finish the shopping. We're busy getting the old chauffeur's quarters ready for Blanca and Henry.

This morning we got pieces of carpet along with some new furniture. You wouldn't believe the cigar stink that was left by some previous smoker. We still need to get drapes and rods, and some paint. The whole place just reeks like an old cigar and it wasn't Cuban," Johnnie said.

Johnnie and Barb discussed the shopping trip in more detail and the plans for Blanca's and Henry's quarters. As they talked, they got refills after all. Johnnie enjoyed being with her friend because she could tell her anything. They had been friends since college; in fact, vivacious Barb had brought the shy Patrick and quiet Johnnie together.

"Just look at the time! We both better get going. Will Blanca be making dinner for you this evening? Or will you be doing your *I Love Lucy* impersonation again. What with all your shopping will you need to soften Patrick up?" Barb asked.

"Oh no, we settled on a budget before I got started and I'm still well within it. We're just going to have leftover pork stir-fry tonight. Maybe I'll make some won tons for an appetizer if I get up from here and go home. Gosh, it was good to talk with you again. Take care, my friend," Johnnie said.

Twelve

When Johnnie got home, she carefully pulled the old cards out of her recipe box and held them gently for a few minutes then decided that if she didn't hear from Linda before Christmas she would take action at that point. She hoped she wouldn't regret waiting.

With her decision made, she prepared the dinner for the evening and waited for Patrick to come home. As they sat together and enjoyed their appetizers, she only sipped from a small glass of Dry Sack with her wontons since she'd already had two glasses of wine. She didn't want a repeat of Sunday night. Johnnie went over the purchases she made that day and the planning that was done on the chauffeur's quarters while they ate dinner. The timing for everything was very tight, but she thought that the Sevilles would be able to move in at least by the Saturday after Thanksgiving, barring any surprises.

"Honey, you've done a great job and even stayed within the budget," Patrick applauded, kissing his wife after dinner.

They decided to make it an early night; even though it was only nine p.m., they were both very tired from their entertaining on Sunday. And since the rest of the week would be busy, they ignored the hour and just went to bed.

Johnnie, having gone to bed so early, rose with the first ray of sun the next day, full of anticipation, as her mother and Colleen would be coming later that day. Blanca would be there for the entire day because she didn't have school until evening on Tuesdays, so Johnnie dressed in causal work clothes and tied her hair up as they would be working hard that day.

"Good morning, Blanca," Johnnie said on seeing her.

"Just take a seat, Mrs. Collins, and I'll bring your breakfast to you. It will be eggs with some home fries, orange juice, toast, and coffee this morning if that sounds good to you."

"It sounds just heavenly, Blanca," Johnnie said.

After breakfast, Johnnie and Blanca went upstairs to the bedrooms to discuss what needed to be done. Once Johnnie got Blanca started making up the rooms, she went downstairs to her office to plan what else she needed to do. She did worry that she wasn't giving Aunt Rose much of her time and decided to call her.

"Hello, Aunt Rose, just thought I'd let you know I'm still among the living," Johnnie greeted her aunt once she got through Sarah, the secretary.

"Oh, Johnnie, it's good to hear from you. I know you're very busy what with everyone coming home for Thanksgiving. Is your mother planning on coming down this year?"

"Yes, Mother will be picked up by Colleen on her way down from school, a little out of her way but not too bad," Johnnie answered.

"Well, I expect all of you around four o'clock Thursday. That should give you enough time for church and whatever else is on your schedules," Rose said.

"We'll be there and are looking forward to it. Philippe always prepares such fine meals; you're very lucky to have him and of course we like seeing Uncle Pete too. Will he be coming?"

"Yes, Pete will be there too. Being a bachelor he doesn't really have much choice," Rose said.

"Aunt Rose, how are things down at the office? Can you stand to have me off till after Thanksgiving?" Johnnie asked.

"Yes, we'll make it till then. But, Johnnie, I do want you to mark your calendar for the Tuesday after Thanksgiving when we will be having our Monthly Management meeting. Bill Stern from manufacturing wants to give us a briefing and I really want all of us to be there," Rose said.

"Okay, Aunt Rose, I've blocked the meeting out on my calendar. Looking forward to Thanksgiving," Johnnie said as she bid her Aunt Rose goodbye.

As she was hanging up the phone, she heard Blanca come in the kitchen.

"Mrs. Collins, Henry is ready to start painting," Blanca announced.

"If you'll go the paint store on Colorado not far from the rug store and close to the Rosemead intersection, we have an account there. I'll call them to let them know you are coming. Henry's moving so quickly; this is great, I think everything is going to turn out just fine."

"Mrs. Collins, can you help with the people from the utilities if they show up while we're gone?" Blanca asked.

"Yes, I'll be here," Johnnie answered.

With that settled, Johnnie went back into her office and called the paint store to give her okay and set up a budget. Then she went over her plans for the various meals she would need to serve to all the company. She was very glad to have Blanca to help; they'd finished the rooms fast with the two of them working. She decided to have Pearl and her girls over one more time before the holiday and called to sign them up for Wednesday, it was really one of her regular days, but she just wanted to confirm. By the time she finished all the planning and phoning, Blanca and Henry were back from the paint store. None of the utility people had shown up during their absence, unfortunately.

"Mrs. Collins, would I be able to help Henry with the painting?" Blanca asked.

"Yes, I have Pearl and her girls coming tomorrow at their regular time. I'll go over what I want them to do with you when you get a chance," Johnnie said.

It was getting near lunchtime, so Johnnie made some salami sandwiches and packed them up with carrot sticks and apples and took them up to the Sevilles. She really just wanted to see what colors they were going to be painting the rooms and didn't want to look like a snoop. Blanca had chosen a sunny yellow for the bedrooms, a rosy cream for the bathroom, and creamy white for the living room, kitchen area, and hallway. Johnnie was very pleased with the choices. Johnnie left them to their labors and promised to pick the drapes and rods after the rooms were painted.

When Johnnie got back into the house, she realized that her mother and Colleen would be there within the hour. She used the back stairs to run up to her bedroom, stopping only briefly in front of her children's pictures, gazing at them lovingly. She showered and washed her hair, then got dressed in a pretty print wool jersey dress that could be worn for dinner as well as afternoon. She let her hair drape elegantly on her shoulders. For jewelry, she wore tasteful dangling earrings of pearls and diamonds. This evening she was in her own house so she wore high heels. She liked to be as tall as her beautiful 5'9" daughter who also liked to wear high heels.

Johnnie just made it downstairs in time to greet her mother and her daughter as they were coming in through the hallway off the kitchen. Colleen was carrying two large unmatched suitcases, one for her and one for her grandmother. She was dressed in her school sweatshirt and jeans with clunky shoes, and looked a little frazzled. Johnnie knew her mom could be a little trying sometimes even though she was as sweet as she could be. Her mom was dressed in a blue dress that went well with her silvery grey hair.

Hugs and kisses were given all around; then the ladies stopped for a moment in the foyer to rest, not that they hadn't been sitting for several hours. Johnnie got her mother some fruit juice to perk her up and gave Colleen some too. Looking at her daughter, Johnnie saw her own heart-shaped face with Patrick's deep blue eyes, and admired her blonde hair, which came from a long line of blondes on both sides. Once refreshed, the ladies stood up to go upstairs.

"Use the elevator, it's in good working order, I had it checked before your visit," Johnnie told Colleen. Johnnie didn't use the elevator herself under any circumstance. The elevator was small and Johnnie got claustrophobic just thinking about it.

Not long after that Ian and Patrick both came, arriving from different locations but at the same time. Now Johnnie had almost all of her family with her and her mom and she was very happy. Scott joined them just before cocktails and everything was perfect. The cocktail hour was delightful, and the dinner of bacon-wrapped chicken and twice baked potatoes, ending with a salad of grapefruit sections and avocado slices on a bed of lettuce with a tangy dressing, was oohed and ahhed over. Patrick chose a Chardonnay for the wine. Blanca prepared the dessert, a wonderful French apple pie, before leaving for school. That night after everyone had gone to bed, Patrick showed his wife, behind closed doors now that the house was full again, just how much he loved her.

Thirteen

Thanksgiving! Johnnie thought as she woke the next morning. Yes, she was very thankful for a lot, her loving husband, her beautiful family, and a host of other things. She got out of bed singing a thanksgiving hymn softly. Patrick was already up and showering, he was singing also. *Guess we're both happy and thankful today,* Johnnie thought as she put on her ruffly pale blue print robe.

While waiting for Patrick to finish, she waltzed downstairs to make some coffee, enough for all her guests. Guests, yes her children were now guests. She was thankful they wanted to come home and not scattered across the country, at least not so far, like the widow Mrs. Malloy's daughter and her own brother Larry who lived in New York.

After fixing the coffee, Johnnie went back upstairs using the beautiful stairs because she just felt like it. Patrick was out of the shower, so Johnnie hopped in to shower and wash her hair. She dressed in a nice flannel pants outfit of smoky gray with a gray-green sweater. She wore a small pair of platinum hoops, a gift from Patrick, and tied her hair, after clipping it, with a coordinating scarf. She wore charcoal gray suede loafers.

"I'm so thankful for you being in my life, Johnnie," Patrick said hugging her and kissing her when she emerged from the dressing area of their bathroom.

"I can't imagine my life without you, Patrick," Johnnie replied as she kissed him back with a tender passion.

"Let's go downstairs and cook something that will get everyone up," Patrick said.

"That's a great idea, Patrick, we'll just leave the kitchen doors open and see if we can't get the smells, hopefully good ones, to waft upstairs," Johnnie said.

Johnnie and Patrick went downstairs and fixed some bacon and French toast, and squeezed some fresh orange juice. It didn't take long before everyone was up and wandering down to the breakfast room. Scott surprised everyone by showing up in time for breakfast. After eating and getting everyone showered and dressed, which always seemed to take a long time even though in this house they had enough bathrooms to accommodate everyone, they went to their church for the Thanksgiving service.

"I'd like to help serve Thanksgiving dinner in the Midnight Mission some time," Ian said as they came out of the service.

"That's really sweet of you, Ian, but the problem will be to get Aunt Rose to agree to it. You know she counts on us for Thanksgiving, not having any family of her own since Uncle Ted passed away," Johnnie said, hugging her son.

"You probably could help them on some other occasion too you know, brother dear," Colleen said bopping the back of her brother's head.

Once home they stretched out in the library and Patrick lit a fire, making the room cozy and comfortable on the gray damp day. Johnnie carried in some coffee and a snack of little sandwiches; she didn't want anyone getting too full before Aunt Rose's dinner. They spent the time sharing what each of them was thankful for. Johnnie was so happy she felt like she was going to pop, so instead she gave her mother a big hug.

"Do you think we could call Larry?" her mother asked plaintively.

"Of course, Mother. Do you want to call here or we could go to my office where you can have privacy if you want?" Johnnie said.

"If I call from here, we can all talk to him and I think he would like that," Iris said.

So they called Larry and each person talked to him but none as long as his mother. Johnnie hoped there wouldn't be tears when she finished, and thankfully, there weren't.

"It was just so good to hear Larry's voice. I miss him so very much," Johnnie's mother said without a tear but with a catch in her voice.

Johnnie was relieved that her mother seemed to be taking it okay that Larry wouldn't be there. He never came home, well, hardly ever. He was a lawyer in New York and worked long hours. He was married to a lady that the family was always polite to but had never warmed up to. She just seemed very cold, as cold as a snowstorm in New York. They had three children, all boys, in various grades of junior high and high school. Her mother hoped that maybe the grandchildren would come out to California to go to college.

"Guess we all should start getting dressed for dinner so we can get there on time. You know how Aunt Rose likes us to arrive an hour before dinner," Johnnie said, stretching as she got up.

"Before everyone separates, let's decide who'll be the designated drivers," Patrick ordered.

"I'll be happy to. You know I don't like Old Fashioneds," Scott said.

"I'll also be happy to drive since I'm too young to drink," Ian said, not to be outdone by his older brother.

Fourteen

After the family got ready to go, no easy task, they decided that Ian would drive the ladies and Scott would just take his father. It wasn't really a long drive at all. Aunt Rose lived in a fine home close to the Wrigley Mansion, now Tournament House for the Tournament of Roses. Johnnie and Patrick lived a few blocks east of the mansion. They had all dressed in some of their finest evening clothes, because Aunt Rose liked to have people dress for her dinners. The men didn't have to wear tuxedos, just a good dark suit. The ladies all wore tasteful gowns, not formal, but certainly dressy.

Johnnie was dressed in a beautiful wool crepe, long-sleeved rose dress with a wrapped bodice and eased straight long skirt. Her belt was encrusted with beads and pearls. In the v of the dress's wrap, she wore a string of grandmother's lovely matched pearls, with a pin of pearls and diamonds in swirls on her shoulder. Her earrings matched the necklace. She had wrapped her hair up in a twisty style and fastened it with a sparkly clip. Patrick wore the black suit that Johnnie liked so well. Her sons, looking just so handsome, were dressed in their best suits. Her daughter Colleen looked stunning in a silk printed dress. Her mother was dressed in a long, flowing gown of a silvery gray color.

"My, don't we all looked so nice, all cleaned up with faces washed," Colleen said.

"Yes, we do make a handsome picture," Patrick said as he hugged Colleen and gave his wife a kiss.

They were at Aunt Rose's sprawling white house in just a few minutes because it was so close. She had a large circular driveway in the front of her house where they parked both cars, leaving plenty of room for Uncle Pete when he arrived from Arcadia. They went as a group up the broad stone stairs through the large portico to the imposing front door. Patrick, leading the pack, rang the doorbell. Mr. Martin, Aunt Rose's butler, answered the door and led the family into a foyer much larger than Johnnie's, where they would have their cocktails, namely Old Fashioneds. No matter how many times Johnnie came over to Aunt Rose's, she always felt intimidated. Today she was glad to have her mother, Aunt Rose's sister, with her.

Their hostess swished into the room in a long black taffeta skirt that rustled when she walked. She wore a silk organza blouse with full puffy long sleeves and a large pointy collar, accessorized with a diamond necklace and earrings. Her hair was in its usual twisty style, but with a sparkly comb holding it up.

Kisses and hugs were given all around, then the cocktails were passed out. Mr. Martin came out of the kitchen with a tray of exquisite canapés. There was a sweet, sticky fruit punch for Ian and anyone else not partaking in the cocktails.

"Oh! It's so good to see you, Iris," Aunt Rose exclaimed as she hugged her sister.

"I've missed you too, Rose. We just don't get together enough with me so far away," Iris said.

"Santa Barbara isn't so far that we couldn't see each other more often. I guess we are just both so busy. But that will change soon, because I'm planning on retiring as of January, 1981," Rose said.

"You are? Rose, that surprises me. I didn't think you would ever leave, that they would carry you out," Iris said.

"I've got a great young man who can take my place," Rose said.

"You do?" Iris replied, looking at her sister with a smile.

"Yes, your grandson and my great nephew, Scott," Rose said giving Iris a big hug.

Uncle Pete danced into the room just at that moment. "My two sisters never looked sweeter."

"Pete, it's good to see you." Iris jumped up to give her brother a kiss, while Rose also gave him a quick peck on the check.

"Well, don't you look good there, brother," Iris said.

Pete, tall and trim, was dressed in a finely tailored suit that matched his blue eyes and went well with his full head of white hair. He had a paisley-print ascot for a tie and a linen handkerchief peeked out from his pocket. He wore a diamond ring. Pete was the oldest of the three at seventy-one and had retired, wealthy from his investments, just a few years back, but he was still good looking and could turn the ladies' heads.

"So what are we drinking, could it be Old Fashioneds made with the very best bourbon?" Pete teased.

"Is something wrong with the Old Fashioned, Pete?" Rose asked, looking sort of hurt.

"No, of course not, dear sister," Pete said as he took the cocktail and belted it down.

Pete was not only tall and good looking, but he filled the large room with his presence. The rest of the group was all used to him and it wouldn't be a family gathering without him. He had been married in his youth but the marriage hadn't lasted and he got divorced, the first in the family, without having any children. Iris was the only one of the siblings who had children, a son and a daughter.

"You might as well hear it from me, Pete, I plan to retire this coming January," Rose announced.

"No, that can't be! Not Rose the great businesswoman. What will you do when you can't go to your company?" Pete asked, not hiding his shock.

"Oh, don't worry about that. I've got it all figured out. I'm going to take a month off right after the holidays to see if I can stand not coming into the office each day," Rose said patting Pete's arm.

"Bet you don't even make it through one month. Say, why don't you and Iris live together? This is a big, big house, you gals could just roll around in here and never run into each other," Pete said, hugging the two sisters.

"I think it's about time we eat," Rose said with a sigh.

With that, they all walked into the dining room in an orderly fashion with boy-girl, boy-girl escorts. They took their seats with Aunt Rose at the head of the table, Uncle Pete to her right and Iris to her left. Scott sat next to his grandmother Iris, Colleen next to Scott, and Ian ended the row. On the other side, Johnnie sat next to Uncle Pete, and Patrick sat next to Johnnie. They always sat in these same seats year after year at the heavy, carved walnut table on heavy, carved walnut chairs. The table had a beautiful lace tablecloth over a fine orange linen tablecloth. There was a horn of plenty spilling out various fall items like Indian corn, gourds, and colored leaves Rose imported from the Northeast. Pale gold candles in heavy crystal holders sat on either side of the elaborate centerpiece.

Greta Martin, wife of James, the butler, served the dinner. It started with butternut squash soup, then the turkey roasted with garlic, sage, and sausage stuffing, and turkey gravy. They also had sweet potatoes with caramelized apples, mashed rutabaga mixed with mashed potatoes, green beans with butter and cream, and a cranberry jelled salad molded in a large turkey mold. There was a large, beautifully arranged relish tray and buttermilk biscuits with herbed butter. For dessert, there was raisin pie and pumpkin pie. There was a light-bodied Bordeaux for the adults who were drinking that evening. The menu hadn't changed for years.

"Philippe made a beautiful meal one more time," Uncle Pete said as he slapped the table shaking the pilgrim-shaped salt and pepper shakers, rattling the Wedgwood china making the Gorham silver clank against the china, and making some of the Waterford crystal goblets wobble.

"Yes, I think it's the best ever," Iris said holding on to her glass.

Johnnie always liked that about her mother, she was so happy and pleased with whatever anyone did for her.

"If everyone is finished, let's retire to the parlor," Aunt Rose said as she got up from her chair.

Johnnie got up slowly and groaned inwardly, knowing that this meant having a sweet after dinner drink. Sure enough, once they reached the beautifully decorated parlor with the heirloom quality furnishings, she saw the cart that held various choices to end the evening. Johnnie chose to have some nocello on ice, Patrick and Uncle Pete decided to have some cognac, and Aunt Rose had cream sherry. Colleen declined any and Scott and Ian being the designated drivers weren't forced to choose.

"This has been such a lovely Thanksgiving, I thank you all for coming. Couldn't have had it without all of you," Aunt Rose said sipping her sherry.

That night when they were safely at home, Patrick let his wife know just how thankful he was behind closed doors.

December

So cares and joys abound, as seasons fleet

King Henry VI, Part II, Act I, W. Shakespeare, 1591

Fifteen

As Johnnie sat in her cheery breakfast nook, listlessly thumbing through the morning paper, she sighed. The house was so quiet now with everyone having left for their own places after the Thanksgiving weekend. Finishing the last of her coffee, she carefully put the paper aside.

"Blanca, I'm going to the library to do my LaBauch reading tutoring then on to the country club to swim some laps," she called out.

Johnnie left to go to the main Pasadena Public Library using Del Mar then she took Los Robles to get to East Walnut Street where the Central Library was located. She never could keep it straight, which streets were one way. After searching out a parking place in another too-small lot, she stopped as usual to admire the building. It was newer than her home, but had been built in the late 1920s by the same architectural firm, Myron Hunt and H.C. Chambers, who also designed the Huntington Library and Occidental College. The building had a tile roof, archways, courtyards, and palm trees making it look like a Spanish hacienda.

She sat in the courtyard to the main entrance to wait for her pupil, Ted Sylvan, a young man who, for whatever reason, was not sent to school by his family when he was a young child, which was never discovered by any agency. He didn't go far in school once he got there; without reading skills, it wasn't long before he dropped out. Now he wanted to improve his life and was working hard to master reading. Johnnie was very proud of the progress he made; and she always emphasized it was his progress, not hers.

"Hello, Cora. How are you doing?" Johnnie called out to an older woman who was hurrying out of the library.

"Oh, Mrs. Collins, have you seen Mrs. Marshall?" Cora asked Johnnie, coming over to the bench she was sitting on.

"I believe she went out of town suddenly. At least that is according to Mr. Marshall," Johnnie said.

"I'm just surprised by that. We had some very firm appointments she didn't keep or call me about," Cora complained.

Johnnie knew that these appointments were very important to keep; it was hard for people to admit they didn't read and discouraging when their tutors just dropped them. Linda and Johnnie took the LaBauch training together and tried to do their tutoring at the same time whenever possible.

"I also left several phone messages for her and nobody called me back," Cora added.

Disturbed by further evidence that something was wrong with Linda, Johnnie was unable to comfort her friend's pupil before she saw her own walking up the library steps.

"Hello there, Ted, I'm over here," Johnnie said, rising and hurrying over. "Nice to see you, Cora."

Johnnie went with Ted to their special place in the library and tutored him with part of her mind on what Cora told her. She forced herself to concentrate on the tutoring and promised herself she would give the news her full attention when she was back in her office.

Upset even though the tutoring went well, Johnnie made her usual wrong turn coming out of the parking lot and ended up passing by City Hall. As long as she was driving that way, she slowed down and looked at the building and its Spanish architecture and thought about how the building was used in the sixties TV show *Mission Impossible*. *Why am I stuck in the sixties?* she thought. She decided it was probably all of her thinking about Lionel and Linda, and the folk singer at the last party popped into her mind, along with the last party.

At home in her little office, sitting at her desk, she took out an old greeting card and started to write all the things that were bothering her on the back of the card. Looking at the list, Johnnie knew no one except her would think it was very important so she put the card in her middle desk drawer and decided she wasn't Miss Marple after all.

Sixteen

Over cocktails that evening, Johnnie discussed her concerns about Aunt Rose's business and the Management Meeting the next day. Patrick put his arm around his wife and pulled her close to him.

"I can't imagine what Bill Stern has planned, but you won't be alone, there will be you and five others besides. That should help keep things under control," Patrick said, trying to comfort her.

They ate a quiet dinner and then went their separate ways, Patrick to his study and Johnnie to the kitchen to clean up. After Johnnie finished in the kitchen, she went to their at-home gym and did her work out on the bars, treadmill, and Solo Flex. She had to admit to herself that she did feel a little better as she got into bed. She never heard Patrick come in and go to bed much later that evening.

Rising with her husband, Johnnie realized with dread that this was Tuesday and the Management Meeting at Aunt Rose's business.

"Good morning, my sweet," Patrick said, drawing Johnnie over for a big hug to go with the kiss. "Please don't worry about the meeting today, darling. Let Scott and Rose take care of whatever Bill Stern has up his sleeve."

With a final kiss, they parted to both get ready for the day. Johnnie showered and washed her hair. She decided to wear a honey beige wool suit and a silk print blouse with cornflowers sprinkled gaily about. She put a choker of pearls at her neck and pearl button earrings with diamond flakes around the edges on her ears. For shoes, she chose some very sensible fine brown leather pumps with a matching brown leather purse. She decided to wear her hair in a bun fastened with a tortoise shell clip.

"Don't you look business-like, and so pretty too," Patrick said coming into the dressing area and giving Johnnie a sweet kiss on her neck.

"Do you think I look too severe, should I soften my hair?" Johnnie asked.

"Never," Patrick said and hugged Johnnie once again, kissing her several more times on her neck.

"Come on, lover, we'd better get breakfast and get out of here or you're going to be late," Johnnie said.

They ate a quick breakfast and parted with a final hug and kiss. Johnnie walked out to her car and felt like it was the longest mile she ever walked even though it was only feet from the house. She just knew this was going to be a grueling day and it was.

Hours and hours later, finally reaching her own driveway, the meeting over at last, Johnnie felt like kissing the ground. After parking the car, she slowly got out and walked carefully to her house. Using the back stairs, she walked up to her bedroom.

"Oh, Mrs. Collins, you're back. Should I start dinner?" Blanca inquired as she stepped out of the bathroom she was cleaning.

"Could you? Oh, that would be great, I have a blasting headache. I'm going to take a bath and then lie down for awhile," Johnnie moaned.

Johnnie trudged to her bedroom, not even stopping to gaze at her children as she made her way into the bathroom. Once in the tub, she thought about the miserable meeting she had endured. Bill Stern, from the manufacturing side, presented an aggressive growth plan for the company and was very insistent on it. The meeting was long, noisy, and contentious. *How would Scott handle this? What would Aunt Rose do?* She herself didn't see anything bad about growth; she just didn't want to grow so fast. After all, things were just starting to pick up and she didn't want to see the company spend a lot of money and get left high and dry. She'd tried to get a few words in at the meeting without success. Now she had a whopper of a headache and was irritated besides. Relaxing in the tub, she decided she would take something for the headache when she got out and lay down just for a little bit. She really wanted to discuss what happened in the meeting with Patrick.

Half an hour later, Johnnie rose slowly from her bed and stretched, walked over to her dresser, picked up Scott's photo, and sighed. She went into the dressing area and chose a cashmere pants and sweater outfit of winter white. She put on a long crystal necklace and some dangling crystal earrings. Her shoes were matching winter white peau de soie high-heeled sandals. She made sure to put on some blush and a soft coral lipstick to give her some color. She was feeling a little better when she walked down the beautiful stairway.

"Honey, are you feeling better?" Patrick had been sitting in the foyer sipping a glass of sherry waiting for Johnnie, and he rose when she entered the room.

Patrick took his lovely wife by her arm and led her into the living room where he and Blanca had set up a nice appetizer of cashew nuts from the Hotel Del Coronado that Patrick brought back from one of his golf tournaments. They were carefully saving these wonderful nuts for a special occasion and Johnnie guessed this was it when she noticed the cashews.

"Here, come sit over here and let me bring you a healing glass of sherry. Blanca has dinner under control so don't worry about a thing," Patrick said pointing to the sofa.

"And why don't you bring those nuts over here too, sweetie. How nice of you to bring them out for me," Johnnie said.

"Oh, nothing is too good for my Johnnie," Patrick said as he nestled in next to Johnnie with the precious bowl of giant cashews.

They made a decision not to discuss business over their delicious dinner of sirloin tip roast, roasted potatoes, green beans almandine, and a green salad. Instead, they reviewed plans of the Christmas parties they would be giving. Johnnie would be having the history department over as she always did for an open house. *At least in this house they'll all fit comfortably,* she thought with a smile.

"It's good to see you smile," Patrick said.

"I was just thinking about how much better everyone from your department fits in this house than our last house. That's all," Johnnie said.

With that, they both laughed and remembered things about their old life in the other house.

"Johnnie, you aren't sorry we moved here, are you?" Patrick asked.

"Oh no, I truly love living here." Johnnie rose, leaned across the table, and kissed her husband.

"Umm, let's go upstairs, my sweet. And no sneaking down to do the dishes, promise," Patrick said.

"Okay, I promise," Johnnie said crossing her heart.

That night was as special as the cashews from the Hotel Del. And Johnnie didn't sneak down to do the dishes, although she did wake in the wee hours of the morning and thought about it.

Seventeen

Johnnie awoke with a song in her heart and a big smile on her face. Patrick was so sweet to her last night she wanted to sing out loud for the whole world to hear. She dressed in Pendleton wool pants of a blue and green plaid and a fuzzy yellow sweater that picked up a thin yellow line in the plaid. She clipped her hair at the neck with a tortoise shell barrette. Walking down the beautiful staircase, she softly sang a Christmas carol.

"Oh the good fairy cleaned the kitchen while we slept," Johnnie said when she saw the clean kitchen.

"It was just me, Mrs. Collins," Blanca said. "Let me bring you some breakfast. Mr. Collins had to leave early this morning but he left you this drink for your headache."

"Yes, Mr. Collins has many different concoctions for various aliments. Bring it over and I'll choke it down. At least he won't see my grimace when I drink it."

"We have a breakfast of warm blueberry muffins, and a hot fruit compote sprinkled with granola. Does that sound okay to you?" Blanca asked.

"It's just what the doctor ordered. We sure like having you here Blanca, and Henry too. You've both been so helpful," Johnnie said as she sipped her coffee after breakfast.

Blanca blushed and murmured a halting thank you.

"We're just so grateful to you and Mr. Collins for taking us in when we really didn't have any place to go. Now we can finish school and make something of ourselves. I'm also thankful to be learning about cooking all these different recipes."

"I'm glad it worked out too, Blanca," Johnnie admitted as she

91

rose from her seat. "Now, I'm off to do some Christmas shopping. I'm taking the day off from work and they already know. After I finish with the shopping, I'm going to the country club to swim some laps, so I probably won't be home till late."

Johnnie drove to Colorado Street to start her shopping at Robinson's Department Store then Vroman's Bookstore. She decided that before she walked to Vroman's, she would wander through Hall's Jewelry and drool over possible gifts that Patrick could give her after she gave him a hint or two. After hitting all those stores, she would go up to Bullock's around lunchtime. She preferred to eat there anyway; no sense eating at Robinson's since they catered to an older crowd and the food was just too bland. After eating, she would shop a little in Bullock's then head for the country club. Shopping list in hand, she parked in the nice roomy lot at Robinson's and started her marathon shopping trip.

She found some lovely gifts for her mother at Robinson's and in the Men's Department she found some beautiful silk ties for all the men in her family, including Uncle Pete who would be with them at Christmas. Then she wandered over to Hall's and peeked at several pieces of jewelry that caught her eye. She saw a watch that she liked and a pearl dinner ring with diamond, ruby, emerald, and sapphire accents. She actually asked to try it on and it was breathtaking. *Well, she thought, this gives Patrick two choices one in our reach and the other probably way out of it. Oh well,* she sighed to herself, *that's not what Christmas is about anyway.*

At Vroman's she wandered around looking at all the interesting books. Johnnie liked to read historical novels, biographies, and true life adventures. She, Linda, and Barb had a book club. The ladies would have the group to their house once a month on a rotating basis, and the one hosting got to choose the book. It would be Johnnie's turn in May when they would be starting up again once there were no more holidays for awhile. Johnnie wondered if Linda would be back by then or at least heard from. She picked out a couple of fun books for the kids and then special ordered the books Patrick had on his list.

It was getting near lunchtime so Johnnie drove over to Bullock's and found a parking space in the tight parking structures. She walked over the bridge and into Bullocks.

"Mrs. Collins, Johnnie," a male voice called.

Turning, Johnnie saw Charles Defoe looking very handsome in a brown tweed sports jacket with a dark green turtleneck that was probably cashmere, but Johnnie wasn't going to touch it to find out. *He is elegantly casual today,* she thought, *so he must not be meeting clients.*

"Hello, Charles. What brings you to Bullocks? Getting an early start on your Christmas shopping?" Johnnie asked.

"Just looking around for now. No matter how long I plan, somehow I always finish at the very last minute," Charles said.

"I've got some sons and a husband that do the same thing. Some day you will all get caught and be down at Thrifty's shopping on Christmas day with all the other late shoppers," Johnnie said smiling.

"Oh, I hope not! I better change my ways before that happens. Say, it's just about lunchtime. Will you join me for lunch?" Charles said taking hold of Johnnie's arm.

"Okay," Johnnie said, not sure how to get out of it. *Besides,* she thought, *I can quiz him about our fund.*

Charles led Johnnie out of Bullocks and down Lake Street to his office and parking lot.

"Great day for a drive, in fact a perfect day," Charles said coming out of Bullocks and onto the sunny street.

What's this all about? Johnnie thought.

"So, where are you taking me?" Johnnie asked as gaily as she could. They were in a very slick black sports car. She didn't know her cars and really didn't care as long as they got her where she wanted to go. She did appreciate that the car was probably very expensive.

"Just to the Peppermill. I like it there and eat there often," Charles said smoothly.

The Peppermill was up on Walnut. They got out at the door and had the valet park the car; it was the only way to handle the parking. Inside was the smell of fine beef.

"Shall we start with cocktails?" Charles asked once they were seated.

"Yes, I'll have a Bloody Mary," Johnnie said, looking around the restaurant and realizing she was just about the only woman there. *Guess it was a place for a businessman's lunch,* she thought to herself.

"As long as I've lived here, I've never come to the Peppermill for lunch. We've had dinner here sometimes but not lunch. The menu looks good," Johnnie said as she read the menu.

Johnnie ended up having the fish of the day special and Charles chose a steak sandwich.

"So how is our fund doing, Charles?"

"I think you will be very happy in a few days," Charles announced, taking Johnnie's hand and gazing intently into her eyes.

"Oh, that's always good news just before Christmas and all," Johnnie said withdrawing her hand as gracefully as possible.

Lunch was delicious, but Johnnie was uncomfortable all the same. After Charles paid the bill with a charge card, they got up to leave and Johnnie felt his hand on her back as they walked out. He dropped her off at Bullocks on the way back but not before he leaned over and kissed her goodbye, a kiss with more passion than Johnnie expected. She didn't know what to think exactly because she didn't like to kiss men that she didn't know well and weren't relatives.

Once safely inside Bullocks, Johnnie had some shopping she wanted to do. Colleen had mentioned some clothes that she had seen that she wanted. Johnnie really liked to have Colleen with her when she bought her clothes, but Colleen gave very explicit descriptions of the items so Johnnie didn't think she would make a mistake. Still she didn't feel very confident when she picked out the items. She didn't know why she felt like this when Colleen was always so gracious and thankful for all her gifts. She actually treasured them. The boys were a totally different proposition; she never felt self conscious about their gifts even though they were fussy. She just didn't understand herself sometimes. *Today is not the day. Oh well, time to swim,* she thought.

Eighteen

As she drove to the county club, she wondered if Barb would be there. She decided to call her once at the club and make an appointment rather than take a chance of running into her. She found Barb at home and willing, in fact eager, to meet her. Johnnie didn't have too much trouble with the pool this time, somehow she just hit it lucky in between the morning and after school swimmers.

"Mrs. Collins, have you thought of entering our swim meet?"

"Oh, hi, Coach Hank. No, I really just swim as a hobby not for training. Those days are gone what with a family to take care of and all. Thanks for asking," Johnnie replied.

"You have such a good form in the water, Mrs. Collins, lots of strength too. I wouldn't think you would need to train too many more hours than you do now," Coach Hank said.

"Well, I'll think about it. When is the meet?" Johnnie asked.

"Not till the end of February, so you'll have time if you decided to enter," Coach Hank answered.

Johnnie missed Linda and their own swim meets in Linda's pool that included lots of laughs. Checking the time as she climbed out of the pool, she saw she had to hurry in order to meet Barb.

"Barb, oh Barb," Johnnie called to her friend who was walking quickly to the juice bar. The ladies had decided not to have cocktails since Johnnie had one at lunch.

"So tell me about the lunch," Barb said excitedly.

"Not much to tell. We went to the Peppermill, had a good lunch and then I was dropped back at Bullocks," Johnnie said.

Barb was not satisfied with Johnnie's answer and kept after her till she had every detail including what they ate and drank, and even the goodbye kiss. Johnnie didn't know what to make of her friend. Why did Barb have such a burning interest in Charles Defoe when she and Stan didn't even invest with him? Why was she so animated? Did Johnnie dare ask? Would she want to hear the answer? *No, Johnnie thought, just leave it alone, probably nothing was happening with Charles and Barb anyway.*

"Look at the time! I better run! I don't have a Blanca cooking my meals," Barb said, getting up quickly.

"Well, she isn't really a cook but it does help a lot having her," Johnnie said as she gathered her swim things.

Johnnie hurried to change her clothes when she got home, into a long wool crepe dress of a deep purple with a fitted bodice and a cowl neckline. She wore diamond cluster earrings and a small diamond-heart pendant inside the cowl neck. She put a gold bangle on her wrist, a gift from Patrick. Her hair was softly waving around her shoulders. Before she changed her clothes, Johnnie stowed her gifts in the upstairs closet of a small, unused room at the end of the hall, the first room from the back stairs landing.

She was just coming down the beautiful staircase when Patrick walked through the hallway off the foyer.

"Johnnie, you look so lovely. Are we having company?" Patrick said as he walked over to his wife to give her a big kiss.

"Only you, my love," Johnnie said, kissing her husband back. Johnnie wondered if she was feeling guilty about her lunch with Charles Defoe.

"Well, let me clean up and I'll be right down," Patrick replied as he walked quickly up the stairs two at a time.

Johnnie went out to the kitchen to see what Blanca had done for dinner. She really was lucky to have Blanca; but she was working hard to feel lucky and not guilty. After all, they chose to live in this big house and it was a lot for one person to take care of.

They had their cocktails in the living room, sitting and watching the setting sun through the picture window.

"Here, try some of these little bites Blanca made for us this evening. She really is getting into cooking," Johnnie said passing a plate of carefully prepared hors d'oeuvres of cucumber slices with sour cream and a little chopped hard-boiled egg, some cherry tomatoes with a filling of deviled ham, broiled dates filled with gruyere cheese and wrapped in bacon.

"She really is doing good things out in that kitchen." Patrick grinned as he sampled everything. "She's not up to your high standard yet, but I think she'll do!"

Then Patrick sat up straight, cleared his throat, and looked very uneasy. "Johnnie, I've got to tell you something about Stan and myself that we've been keeping a secret. I'm afraid Stan told Barb, so I think it's only fair I tell you unless Barb's already told you."

"Told me what? We didn't talk about you and Stan this afternoon," Johnnie said.

Johnnie was silently thinking about what they did talk about, hoping it wasn't showing on her face. She didn't know what to make of this. She was the one with something to confess and she squirmed in her seat feeling like a little kid with a secret.

"Stan and I are writing a historical novel based on the civil war…and it won't be competing against *Gone With the Wind*. We aren't using our names and we don't want the department to know about the book. It's not going to be any Pulitzer Prize-winner so we really don't want to share it with the department," Patrick said all in one breath.

"Oh, Patrick, I think that's just wonderful! You know how much I like historical novels. Can I help, proofread, what can I do?" Johnnie asked.

Patrick blushed and took a large sip of his drink. "I'm glad you're not disappointed in me."

"Disappointed, why? Because it won't be the book of the century? It could be, you know," Johnnie said.

"We just want to write a best seller that's all. Probably that's asking a lot. I don't know. Anyway, you know Stan, everything in the book has to be historically correct. So right now, we are in the planning stages. We're going to be meeting on campus after classes on Thursdays and even eating dinner there. Will this be all right with you?" Patrick said.

"Of course, take all the time you need, just come home to me, sweetie," Johnnie said, snuggling up to Patrick and thinking she better keep her secret, after all everything happened in innocence on her part.

That night after the roasted chicken dinner Blanca prepared for them, Patrick let his wife know just how much he appreciated her support.

Nineteen

The next morning, as a Christmas carol rang in her head, Johnnie decided to start her Christmas decorating as she sipped her coffee after breakfast. She was dressed in brown corduroy pants and a rose sweater that had a large cowl neck folded over and resting on her shoulders. Her hair was in a ponytail at her neckline. She knew she should probably go into work but she just couldn't yet. She needed to wait a few days and let the dust settle after the Management Meeting. Aunt Rose would call if she was needed desperately, she always did. But with Scott working there, the calls weren't so often or so insistent.

"Blanca, oh Blanca," Johnnie called after deciding to stay home.

"Yes, Mrs. Collins, what can I do for you?"

"After Pearl and her girls finish, would you like to help me with the Christmas decorations? I've decided it's about time this house started to look like Christmas is coming," Johnnie said.

"Oh, that will be fun, Mrs. Collins," Blanca said.

Johnnie climbed the back stairs because the landing behind the small room where she hid the presents was a large storage area. The former owners had made the area nice with shelves and good lighting. Johnnie decided to put the boxes in the elevator and send it downstairs, then she and Blanca could unload them. The boxes would go down unescorted because Johnnie, being claustrophobic, was not going to even step into the elevator, she was just going to push the boxes in from the opening and that was that. She moved the boxes in two stages, getting a pile at the corner before the elevator, that way she wouldn't wear herself before she even started decorating, at least that's what she hoped.

While she was in the storage room, she opened some of the boxes just to check and make sure the contents matched the labels. She sighed when she opened the box full of ornaments her children had made her so long ago. She looked lovingly at the ornaments that her grandmother had used and was so glad her mother let her have them. They didn't even discuss it with her brother because he was so far away.

Larry, she thought. Maybe she would call him, see if she could get him and his family out for Christmas or maybe after Christmas, and even have them stay for New Year's Day. *After all, we have a world class parade on New Year's Day.* She knew how much her mother pined for Larry, especially at holiday time. Yes, she would discuss having Larry and family out with Patrick tonight she decided. Then she got the Christmas tree out and shoved it down the hallway.

After Blanca and Johnnie got the elevator cleared out on the first floor and the boxes moved to the foyer, they decided to rest and have a little snack. Johnnie made some coffee and Blanca made some cheese and crackers and some cut up fruit. After the snack they felt revived and began to set up the tree.

"Oh, you have an artificial tree, Mrs. Collins," Blanca observed.

"Yes, I like to keep the tree up a long time and we don't want to worry about fire or dropping needles. Besides, we all breathe easier with the artificial tree. I'll get a pine wreath for the front door," Johnnie said.

The women struggled with the awkward pieces of the tree. Johnnie was glad she worked out on the Solo Flex as she muscled the large tree into place.

"There now, we can start decorating the tree once we catch our breath," Johnnie said breathing hard. Setting up the tree went a lot easier when the men of the house did it but she didn't want to wait; besides Patrick was the only man in the house now.

After the ladies studied their handiwork for a moment, they began to decorate the tree. They grouped the boxes together that held all the ornaments. Johnnie arranged the boxes in the order she wanted to put them on the tree. She had labeled the boxes long ago so she could put the ornaments on in a certain order. First went the lights.

"Guess we'll have to hold the top piece till Patrick gets home along with these particular ornaments I want on the top branches. I don't like getting on a ladder and reaching in—the branches are prickly," Johnnie told Blanca as she got the ornaments out and laid them on the nearby credenza.

"These are all such beautiful ornaments. They're like the ones my grandmother has on her tree only even more beautiful. I believe they are mouth blown glass ornaments from Europe." Blanca seemed awestruck by the elegance of the ornaments.

"The really nice ones were my late grandmother's and really are very fine examples from Europe. I love having them and treasure them. That's why the tree is in this corner in the foyer, where no one walks. I would hate to have anything happen to them."

After decorating the tree, the ladies strung an artificial pine garland along the banister of the beautiful staircase and then tied some ornaments and festive bows to the garland. They put some Christmas figures like Santa Claus and Christmas mice around in strategic places and scattered some other Christmas decorations on the various tables and other places in the foyer. Then they stood back and admired their work.

"Yes, this is a good start in getting our house decorated for Christmas. We'll have the bar and hors d'oeuvres out here in the foyer for the Department Open House. Now we need to fix up the living room. Our guests will be milling in there also but they won't be going in the rest of the house; maybe I'll ask Henry to serve as security. It's really a nice bunch so it won't be stressful for him. Oh, and we'll need to decorate the hall bathroom also," Johnnie said.

"I'm sure Henry won't mind. Did you have something in mind for me? And when is the party again?" Blanca said.

"The party is next Friday from four to whenever. I hope your schedule will allow you to help me with it.," Johnnie said.

"Oh, yes, absolutely," Blanca said.

"I'm hiring a caterer for the party but I do want to bake some cookies this weekend and you can help me if you want. That night, I would like you to take care of the caterers and make sure everything goes smoothly. I'll be helping, of course, but I really need to spend time with the guests," Johnnie said.

"I'll check my school commitments, but I'm pretty sure I can help with the cookie baking and sure want to. I'm just getting such good experience here, Mrs. Collins," Blanca said.

With everything settled, the ladies decorated the living room and bathroom so that the party rooms looked ready. They decided to wait on doing anything with the rest of the house till another day. Johnnie took off to go swimming and Blanca went to her class.

Twenty

They enjoyed a lovely dinner of sautéed pork chops with mustard, capers, and cream that evening, and Johnnie presented her plan to call Larry.

"Yes, I think that's an excellent plan. Let's convert the bedroom on the first floor back into a bedroom. We'll have the exercise equipment moved to the small bedroom by the landing of the back stairs. Your mother would prefer to be on the first floor no matter what. She doesn't like the elevator any more than you do my love," Patrick said, taking Johnnie's hand.

"Do you think we can call now? I know it's late back east, but I'll bet Larry is just coming home," Johnnie asked.

So, they made the call and actually caught Larry, surprisingly enough. He told them he would seriously consider the trip after Johnnie let him know just how much their mother missed him and his family.

"Now that that's all set, let's go to bed, sweetheart," Patrick said pulling his wife towards their bedroom.

Once again they were going to bed with the dishes not finished. This time Johnnie made no promises about letting the kitchen go. So in the wee hours of the morning she got up very quietly and cleaned the kitchen the way she liked to have it. As she worked, she thought about Larry and hoped with all her heart he would come to visit. It would really make a wonderful Christmas for her mother. By the time she finished with the kitchen, it was almost time for Patrick to get up so she went back upstairs and changed into a very fluffy, semi-sheer pale blue negligee with matching robe and high heeled pale blue slippers with feathers on the toes.

She was working in the kitchen making coffee and a breakfast of some fresh baked blueberry muffins, soft-boiled eggs, and orange juice.

"I am a lucky man. Not only do I have the most beautiful wife but she can cook too." Patrick looked pleased as he strolled into the kitchen and hugged his wife passionately.

They ate their breakfast sitting cozily together in the cheery breakfast room.

"Johnnie, I want to skip my first class, my assistant can run it. Let's go back upstairs," Patrick whispered to his wife.

Patrick missed his morning class for the first time that semester and Johnnie didn't clean the kitchen after breakfast.

"Mrs. Collins," Blanca knocked on the bedroom door.

Johnnie was sleeping a little late after Patrick left to catch his next class. She stretched luxuriously and rolled over but the knocking wasn't stopping.

"Come in, Blanca," she called to her housekeeper.

"Sorry, Mrs. Collins, but weren't you going to work today?" Blanca asked.

"Oh my gosh! Yes, I am," Johnnie said jumping out of bed and quickly getting dressed for work.

She decided on a business look and wore a navy blue wool gabardine suit with a beige blouse with pinks and yellows in the print. She wore simple gold earrings and a gold bangle bracelet, a present from Patrick. Her hair was pinned up and back at the sides, leaving the back in soft waves to her shoulders. She wore simple navy pumps and carried a navy purse.

Driving down Huntington Drive to her Aunt Rose's business, she hummed to herself, happy that her man loved her so. She really was lucky having such a fine, loving husband. She went into work with a foolish grin on her face singing a Christmas carol softly.

"Johnnie, you certainly look like someone with a big secret," Aunt Rose teased on seeing her niece.

"Oh, Aunt Rose, I've called Larry and he just might come out for Christmas with his family," Johnnie interjected quickly, certainly not wanting to tell her Aunt what she actually was smiling about.

"That's just great. I know Iris will be tickled," Rose said smiling.

"Please don't say anything yet because I don't have his final answer," Johnnie said.

The rest of the day went okay. A small group had been set up to recommend what the company would do about Bill Stern's expansion plan. Having formed this group and giving it a deadline placated Bill, so things were quiet around the office.

"Johnnie, I know you do a lot of entertaining at Christmas and lots of other stuff; so since we aren't super busy why don't you take the rest of the year off?" Rose offered as they were preparing to leave that night.

"Okay! That's a lovely idea, Aunt Rose. But be sure to call me if you need me," Johnnie said, knowing her Aunt would call only in a dire emergency.

Twenty-one

A big surprise was waiting when Johnnie returned home that evening. Mixed in with a large pile of Christmas cards was a letter postmarked in Carlsbad, California. Since she didn't know anyone in Carlsbad, she was puzzled. She dropped the rest of the mail on the credenza in the foyer and sat at the chair next to it. Opening the letter, she noticed something odd: the salutation was hand written, but the rest was typed, all except for the signature, which was Linda Marshall. A short hand written note was smeared at the end but Johnnie could only make out some of the words—see, maybe, soon. The Christmas letter gave details about what Linda and Lionel had done during the year and that she was writing from Carlsbad. She didn't say why she was there or when she was coming back. Johnnie couldn't tell for sure if the handwriting was Linda's or not because her friend didn't have very distinctive handwriting and there wasn't much of it.

One thing did bother Johnnie a little about the letter and she circled it. She knew they'd gone to Perris a few years back, and Johnnie couldn't figure out why Linda had included the trip in her letter. There was no return address so she couldn't ask her. The Christmas letter gave her hope but made her uneasy at the same time. She decided to go through with her plan for the Golfer's Christmas party even though she'd heard from Linda or had she? *But why would anyone want to write a letter for Linda,* Johnnie thought, disgusted with herself. She carefully saved the letter in her desk drawer to study thoroughly when she had more time. Maybe she would even discuss it with Barb and risk being called Miss Marple.

The next few days just flew. They got a call from Larry saying the family would be out after Christmas. They'd fly into LAX on December twenty-seventh and stay through January second. Everyone in the California family, especially Iris and Rose, were ecstatic about the impending visit. Patrick arranged to get the rooms switched so that the downstairs bedroom was reinstated.

"Mrs. Collins, there's a phone call for you. It's Mrs. Stevens," Blanca announced after finding Johnnie rummaging around in the upstairs storage room.

Johnnie dusted herself off and hurried to the phone.

"So, what are we doing for dinner this evening?" Barb asked when Johnnie answered the phone.

"Barb! Don't know; do you have any ideas? After all, we're free tonight with our guys working on their book," Johnnie said.

"I've just got such a taste for ribs. Want to go to the Cheyenne Supper Club?" Barb said.

"That does sound good and we won't have to worry about the Santa Anita crowd because the horses haven't started to run yet. I'll just need to clean up; when I'm ready I'll pick you up," Johnnie volunteered.

"Don't be silly, I'll come over and wait," Barb said.

Johnnie walked down the hall to her bedroom, after telling Blanca she wouldn't be home for dinner. She showered quickly, then dressed in a pantsuit of royal blue with a blouse striped in royal blue, purple, green, and white. She fastened a small gold pin of an antique jug on her lapel, and added small gold earrings with diamond accents, a present from Patrick. Johnnie twisted her hair up and fastened it with a tortoise shell comb. She put on high navy pumps, checked herself in the mirror and considered herself ready. She walked down the back stairs and went to her office to retrieve the Christmas letter from Linda just in case she gathered the courage to discuss it with Barb. About the time she walked out of her office, Barb rang the doorbell.

"I'll get the door, Blanca," Johnnie called out.

The ladies laughed as they drove over to Arcadia and the Cheyenne Supper Club.

"I'm glad we didn't wait any longer to get here. Did you see the crowd behind us?" Barb giggled as the ladies sat sipping their cocktails.

Johnnie had a martini, and Barb was drinking Scotch and water. Johnnie was taking her time and not matching Barb drink for drink because she now knew better; besides, she was driving. They munched on an appetizer of fried zucchini as they sipped their cocktails.

"Oh, Johnnie, did I tell you we got a Christmas card from Charles Defoe?" Barb inquired, blushing and fiddling with her cocktail.

"Yes, we got a card from Charles, too, but what we're waiting for is the dividend check," Johnnie said.

"Didn't you think it was just the most beautiful card? He even included a short note to us. Wasn't that nice of him when we're not even investors?" Barb gushed.

"Yes, Charles does have a way about him," Johnnie agreed reluctantly.

"Are you still sore about that goodbye kiss?" Barb asked.

"No, just getting antsy about the expected check," Johnnie answered slowly.

Johnnie thought her friend was a little too excited about the card from the great Charles Defoe and wondered what was she was up to. To change the subject she brought out the Christmas letter from Linda. "Did you get a letter from Linda?"

"Ah, yes we did, it was good to hear from her," Barb said with a big smile.

"Did you notice anything out of the ordinary in the letter, Barb?" Johnnie said tentatively.

"Like what?" Barb took another swig of her drink and began looking around for the waitress.

"Well, this part about their trip to Perris when they got the wonderful potatoes from a roadside stand is troubling to me. I know the Marshals went to Perris in 1978 and got some great potatoes that Linda bragged about for a few months. She even fixed a potato salad with those potatoes for a barbeque we attended at her house. Do you

108

remember those potatoes?" Johnnie said.

"Yes, but I don't see the significance," Barb said impatiently. Before Johnnie could answer, their barbequed pork ribs, steak fries, and coleslaw were served, so they had to wait to continue the discussion. Actually, the ladies were quiet for a while as they enjoyed the delicious dinner.

"Oh, they do make good ribs here," Barb said as she finished. She used the packaged wet towels to clean her hands and Johnnie did too.

"Yes, dinner really hit the spot. Wonder what the guys are eating?" Johnnie said.

"I know I'll hear all about it and all about the complaints too," Barb said as she signaled the waitress to bring some coffee.

"Well, I'll have to drag it out of Patrick. He doesn't talk much about his work," Johnnie said.

As they drank their coffee, Johnnie wondered if she dare bring up Linda again and decided against it. Barb was just too interested in the card from Charles to focus on the strange letter.

"Johnnie, don't make too much of Linda's Christmas letter. There could be all kinds of reasons for those potatoes; maybe they even went again this year before she took off. It was good to hear from her and let's leave it at that," Barb said as Johnnie was dropping her off.

"You're probably right, Barb," Johnnie replied, glad she hadn't been the one to bring it up.

Once she was back in her house, she put the letter back in her desk drawer, not knowing if she was really ready to just "leave it at that." She took out her "Linda list" and added the potatoes. *Well, there's nothing I can do to find her tonight but maybe a bubble bath will clear my mind,* she decided.

After her relaxing soak, she donned a frilly white negligee and matching robe, with a pair of white satin ballet slippers. Then she went downstairs to the family room to wait for Patrick, fixing herself a glass of sherry.

"Oh, I don't how much more I can take of this," Patrick said as he dragged himself in through the family room.

Putting his brief case down, he walked over to his wife and gave her a big hug and long kiss. Then they walked arm in arm down to Patrick's study.

"Did you get enough to eat? Would you like me to fix you a sandwich?" Johnnie asked.

"That would be great, though I could use a Scotch and water, too. Maybe even a double. I don't want to pick on Stan, but he's going into way too much detail. After all, we're writing fiction so we just need to get the general history correct. We're making up the people. I like research as much as anybody but we'll never finish at this rate," Patrick said.

Johnnie gave her husband a nice kiss and went to the kitchen to make the sandwich while Patrick cleaned up. She hoped the men could work out their differences; Barb was so excited about the project and proud of Stan, Johnnie would hate to see the project blowup.

Twenty-two

Johnnie leaned against the door of the downstairs bedroom, surveying the mess left when the moving men finished moving all the gym equipment upstairs. The bedroom was okay, but it lacked something, it still needed some homey touches. It was hard to make up the room around the bar and mirror configuration, which they could not take down, so she decided to put the bed in front of it when it was delivered. The two nightstands would sit on either side of the bed. The tall dresser was in the large closet. She needed to get some lamps for the nightstands and an easy chair with a little table or lady's desk for the corner. That would finish the guest room nicely.

As she drove up Colorado Street, she decided to start with Robinson's. She had a certain style and color in mind, which would probably make it harder to find. After most of an hour searching, she realized that none of the occasional chairs suited her, even though they were all very nice. She found some beautiful brass lamps, though, and arranged to have them delivered.

Next, she went to Bullock's and found just the desk that she wanted. It even would coordinate with the pecan wood bedroom furniture. She picked up some extra sheets, blankets, and a pretty green, blue, and aqua plaid comforter, her mother's favorite colors.

Her last stop was Barker Brothers to see if she could find the chair that was so clear in her mind. Fortunately for her poor, tired feet, she struck gold, literally, when she found the perfect side chair with blue upholstery and gold accented arms that would coordinate nicely with the comforter.

Furniture shopping finished, she went to the El Rancho to get the ingredients for the Saturday cookie baking so they could prepare and freeze the dough, then bake closer to the parties. Johnnie liked to do that each holiday season because it was one less thing to worry about.

After grocery shopping, checking her watch, she decided there was enough time to swim some laps and give Coach Hank his answer. She was eager to participate in the swim meet in February and hoped she would not regret it.

Coach Hank was excited to have Johnnie join the team and introduced her to the members practicing that day. Johnnie was glad she'd only be the third oldest. Everyone she met was pleased to have her on the team. She wondered if they had seen her swim or if Coach Hank had bragged too much.

Twenty-three

Early that Saturday, Johnnie and Blanca got started in the kitchen. They began by making various cookie doughs and fudge, then segued into candied and spiced nuts, and candied orange and grapefruit peel. They spent the greater part of the afternoon finishing some of the more elaborate cookies that used different kinds of dough to made patterns. The ladies were tired after all that work, so they put a simple roast in the oven for dinner. Looking forward to some quiet time, Johnnie sent Blanca to her quarters and took herself upstairs for a relaxing bubble bath.

The brass lamps were delivered before Johnnie could go upstairs. She thought that the plain linen shades looked just right when she saw them on the two nightstands and was glad she'd decided against the pleated ones. Forgoing the pleasures of her relaxing soak, she brought some Christmas decorations into the room to make the room festive for her mother. As soon as the bed arrived and she could make it up, the room would really start to shape up. She hoped the bar and mirror would disappear.

Friday, it's Friday already the day of the open house, Johnnie thought, waking with a start. She got up quietly, not wanting to disturb Patrick who was still sleeping peacefully next to her. He looked so sweet that she wanted to kiss him, so she did very softly. She took a quick shower and dressed in work clothes of black jeans, beaded belt, and a cobalt blue turtleneck shirt. She tied her hair up in a printed scarf of blues and blacks.

Downstairs, she started a pot of coffee then went to her office to get her schedule for the day. Pearl and her girls had already worked very hard to make the house sparkle. Yesterday, Johnnie and Blanca baked a dizzying variety of cookies and arranged them on trays before covering them very well. The fudge, nuts, and candied peels were also arranged on trays and ready to be set out. Patrick had already chosen the music that would be played when the High Notes took their breaks. All that was left was the caterer, who would arrive at ten a.m. to setup and cook. The flowers and Christmas greens were to be delivered at two, and Johnnie would dress for the party after the flowers were delivered. That left plenty of time to check everything carefully after she finished her toilette. The High Notes were to set up at three-thirty p.m. and she would check everything again. Just before four o'clock, dressed and downstairs, she would check once more. You could never be too careful when hosting a party!

Johnnie felt a twinge of excitement as she read the schedule. She decided on a quick breakfast of cereal, toast, and juice, then sang softly to herself as she prepared the meal.

"Oh, my Johnnie's in a happy mood this morning," Patrick teased, grabbing his wife and twirling her around the kitchen. "I know this party is going to be the best one yet, my love. I'll be home quickly this afternoon to help however I can," Patrick said.

"Thanks, Patrick. I always like to have your help with this group," Johnnie said.

"I'm a lucky man whose wife will throw such a party for him," Patrick said kissing his wife passionately.

"Let's eat breakfast so you can get off to class and return quickly," Johnnie said, pulling away and bringing the breakfast to the table.

After breakfast, Johnnie and Blanca made a survey of the party rooms making sure there was enough toilet paper in the bathroom, along with soap and fresh hand towels. She carefully planted some tissue boxes around the rooms just in case. Then they prepared some bowls of nuts and mints to place around handy for nibbling.

"Mrs. Collins, how do you want me to dress today: a uniform or a dress?" Blanca asked.

"Henry should wear a dark suit and if you could wear a pretty party dress that would be just fine," Johnnie said.

114

"Okay, I'll tell Henry," Blanca said.

"I'd like you both to be here, dressed and ready, at three o'clock on the dot," Johnnie said smiling.

The kitchen buzzer sounded, announcing the caterer and his crew. Blanca got them set up in the kitchen while Johnnie went over where she wanted the tables and chairs with some of the crew. They had moved the credenzas and various chairs out of the foyer so it was an open room. Now, the plan was to set up a number of small tables and chairs around the foyer, with the food on tables against the north wall. The High Notes would play in front of the Christmas tree, far enough away from it so they couldn't fall on it. Johnnie wanted the combo there to protect the tree; there had been an embarrassing incident involving Patrick's department head a few years back, and she didn't want any repeats.

After getting the foyer set up just the way she wanted it, Johnnie went to the kitchen to see how Blanca was fairing. She went over the menu one more time with the caterer. There would be carpaccio on French bread, a cheese and cracker plate, a vegetable tray with dill dip, sliced baked ham, turkey, and stuffed chicken, potatoes au gratin, vegetable frittata, tricolor pasta salad, and salmon mousse with cucumber sauce. There would be an open bar with soft drinks for those not drinking. Johnnie liked to have the soft drinks served like a cocktail so it wouldn't be obvious who was not imbibing. Neither she nor Patrick would be drinking so they could drive anyone home who needed it.

The flowers arrived just at two p.m. There were centerpieces of Christmas greens and bowls of red and white roses. There were also a couple of sprays to be placed at the edges of the hallway arch.

After taking care of the flowers, Johnnie went upstairs to dress. She took a quick shower and washed her hair. Her dress for the evening was a new, ballerina-length cocktail dress, Kelly green to go with her eyes. The bodice was fitted and had cap sleeves, with a square neckline that wasn't too deep. The skirt billowed out from the fitted waistline and was held out by a stiff under slip, held in place by a fancy belt encrusted with rhinestones. The material of the dress was a silk taffeta, which rustled when Johnnie walked. She liked the dress quite a bit and had paid a little more than she intended so she would be wearing it all season. She decided on a gold pendant with rubies and diamonds that would fit nicely in the squared V of the dress. Her earrings were gold hoops with rubies and diamonds, and she added the gold bangle that Patrick had given her. Just as she was fixing her hair in an up sweep Patrick came in.

"Johnnie, you will be the most beautiful woman at the party," Patrick said whistling.

"Patrick, I'm so glad you're home." Johnnie kissed and hugged her husband gently, so as not to muss her makeup.

"I'll get dressed in a hurry and be downstairs to help you my love," Patrick said kissing his wife one more time.

Johnnie finished fixing her hair, check her appearance, put a dab of Channel twenty-two on her pressure points and sighed, pulled herself together, and decided to make a grand entrance for no one in particular and used the beautiful staircase, walking down it slowly and deliberately in her high heeled sandals.

"Oh, Mrs. Collins, you really are beautiful," Blanca gushed as Johnnie made her entrance.

"Thank you, Blanca," Johnnie said. "You look very nice yourself. Don't we look festive, you in your red and me in my green?"

Johnnie checked the bar to be sure the bartender had everything he needed, then she checked the buffet table and the rooms they would be partying in.

"Is everything okay, madam?" The caterer asked nervously as Johnnie made her third trip through the foyer.

"Everything looks just wonderful and smells delicious too."

Patrick came down in the dark suit that Johnnie liked on him and she gave him a quick squeeze. The guests started to arrive, the High Notes began to play, and the house filled with the happy buzz of the party.

Johnnie was standing in the archway, studying whether they needed anything, when she was grabbed and kissed right on the mouth.

"Professor Waltham, what are you doing?!?" Johnnie exclaimed as she pulled away from him.

"It's the mistletoe. You're right under it," Professor pointed out.

"Henry, could you get this mistletoe down and get rid of it please. Thank you." Further crises averted, Johnnie continued on with more pleasant hostess duties.

The party went along just fine after the mistletoe was removed. Johnnie and Patrick danced along with a few others as the party was in full swing. Scott came by close to the end of the evening to help drive any tipsy guests home and to have some of the good food. People finally started to leave around eleven-thirty p.m. and there was a flurry deciding who could drive and who couldn't. Only three people needed rides, which was great. It worked out so that Scott, Henry, and Patrick could take care of the driving, leaving Johnnie to walk Stan and Barb across the street.

"Johnnie, that was another great Christmas party," Barb said as they got to their door and Johnnie opened it for them.

"Yes, it was a great party, Johnnie. Tell Patrick we thank him for it," Stan said as he stumbled into his house.

"Don't worry about Stan, I'll take care of him," Barb told Johnnie. "Just be careful going back across the street. I'll watch you from my doorway."

Johnnie walked across the street lightly, glad to have the party over. Despite the fact that she had a wonderful time, she still felt the pressure of having Patrick's colleagues over, although most of them were very nice.

The caterers were busy packing up when Johnnie got back into the house. "Everything was very nice and things went smoothly. Thank you very much for your help," Johnnie told the caterer as she paid him.

"It was our pleasure, madam. You have a very nice kitchen to work in and the party rooms were a good size for setting up. We'll be out of here in just a few more minutes."

Johnnie thanked Blanca and paid her also, as any special occasions were to be paid separately.

"Thank you, Mrs. Collins. It really was a lovely party and everyone was so nice. It was a pleasure to be here," Blanca murmured, yawning a little.

When Patrick, Scott, and Henry got back they all separated and each went to their respective bedrooms, as it was late. Patrick and Johnnie slept late the next morning, snuggled up against each other.

Twenty-four

"Oh! The bed to the downstairs bedroom is arriving today," Johnnie said as she woke with a start.

"That's okay, Johnnie, it's still early," Patrick said pulling his wife back in bed. He wanted to show her just how grateful he was for the wonderful party.

Later that morning the bed did arrive and Johnnie finished decorating the room with the new sheets and comforter. She stood back, looked at the room, and decided it would do. She felt like singing out loud, very loud, she was so happy. Patrick really knew how to show appreciation.

Before Johnnie had a chance to decide how to spend the rest of her afternoon, she was called in to Aunt Rose's to go over some figures, even though it was Saturday, which took most of the afternoon. Johnnie came home late and very tired. *Good thing Blanca is making dinner tonight,* she thought as she dragged herself in. Everything smelled wonderful as she walked past the kitchen. She decided to take a quick run on the treadmill to wake up before going down to dinner. Before going upstairs, she checked the mail and saw there was a letter from Charles Defoe. She could hardly contain herself as she carefully opened the letter. In it was a very nice check, just under 20% of the first investment of $25,000. *Wait till Patrick sees this,* she thought as she zipped upstairs, no longer needing the treadmill.

Refreshed after a brisk shower, Johnnie brought the check back downstairs. Patrick was in the living room fixing the cocktails and snacks for the evening.

"Patrick," Johnnie cried, kissing her husband excitedly.

"What? What is it, Johnnie?" Patrick asked, catching her excitement.

"The check, we got the check from Charles Defoe!" Johnnie exclaimed.

"This is just great. Let's put it back in the 'just-in-case' account. It's just great." Patrick said kissing, hugging, and twirling Johnnie around the room. "You know George and Carol Hampton refinanced their house so they could invest. I'm glad it's working out for all of us."

"You mean the Hamptons, who have always given us the business about the interest rate and taxes we pay, refinanced? They must really be paying a big interest now. And they lost their Prop thirteen property tax advantage. I can't believe they did that. They must really believe in this investment," Johnnie said.

Johnnie was still thinking about the Hamptons, Sunday morning after church, while sitting in her office going over the plans for the Golfer's Party that they would give the next Friday. It would be a very special party, because she was determined to put her plan in place and see just what Lionel would do. She hadn't shared the plan with anyone so no one could spoil it. She got out the old recipe cards and carefully copied the recipes into her own notebook. Then she went upstairs and hid the recipe cards in the far corner of one of the shelves of the linen closet feeling slightly paranoid.

Back downstairs, she found Blanca and they checked the downstairs bedroom one more time before Johnnie's mother came to town that day. Iris would be staying for a while because Larry would be there. Johnnie hadn't told her mother about Larry yet, she just asked her to stay through New Year's this time. She never understood why her mother rushed off right after Christmas anyway.

Colleen and her grandmother arrived in the late afternoon, looking frazzled. Johnnie felt a little guilty when she saw her daughter's face.

"The traffic was just horrible. There was a big five-car accident, with a sigalert, and four of the five lanes were closed. I'm pooped," Colleen announced, collapsing into a nearby chair in the foyer.

"Blanca, could you get a snack and some fruit juice for the ladies? And I'll see if Henry can bring in the suitcases. Mother, I have a surprise for you, you're going to be in the downstairs bedroom, the one we used for a gym. We moved the gym upstairs where it is much handier."

"Johnnie, that's great. I don't like the elevator any more than you do," Iris said.

Johnnie and Blanca got the ladies settled in their rooms not telling either that Larry and family were coming out after Christmas. That way, if he didn't show up they wouldn't be disappointed, but Johnnie would never speak to her brother again.

Twenty-five

Johnnie shivered with anticipation as she stepped out of her bubble bath. In a few hours, the golfers would be here for their Christmas party. She didn't have the nerve to ask Lionel if he was bringing the "Babe" with him or not. She and Blanca were just going to quietly put another setting on the table if the woman showed up. Colleen and Iris decided to eat dinner in the breakfast room, as they weren't ready to socialize, though they would dress and greet the guests before disappearing.

Blanca and Johnnie worked hard on the special menu. The day before, they made the dessert of coconut rum flan and almond crisps. During the morning, they prepared a chicken filling for the puff pastry they had cooked the night before and saved carefully. A vegetable tray with carrots, celery, raw small mushrooms, broccoli flowerets, endive leaves, and jicama slices was laid out attractively and carefully wrapped. The green goddess mayonnaise was prepared to be loaded into a hollowed-out red cabbage. Johnnie hadn't made homemade mayonnaise before but she followed the directions carefully and everything turned out okay and sure tasted good when she sampled it. Patrick would take care of the cocktails, but Johnnie needed to make sure that he had everything he would need and worked off a list she had from the hidden recipe cards.

The first course of deviled crab had also been made the day before and carefully stored. They would need to add three to five minutes to the baking time. The green salad was ready to be tossed with the mustard tarragon dressing at the table. The cheese, fruit, and cracker tray was arranged for the after dinner drinks. After checking on the supplies, Johnnie began preparing the cipollini onions that would complement the main course. The beef tenderloin would go in the oven just after the guests arrived and hopefully no one would be over an hour late. That would be rude, after all.

Blanca would cook the cauliflower with Tuscan ragout, the glazed carrots in meat stock, and the lemon roasted potatoes, which would be baked in the second oven needing a high temperature, while they were having cocktails and the first course. All the timing was laid out on the worn recipe cards that Johnnie had carefully copied into her own notebook. Johnnie never felt so organized.

She decided to wear the green cocktail dress, back from the cleaners, with a pearl and diamond necklace, matching earrings, and a pin that she wore on her shoulder. She pulled her hair back at the sides with sparkly combs, and slipped into some high black peau de soie pumps with sparkling clips. She changed the belt from the one encrusted with rhinestones to a printed one with green, purple, and gold threads. It came up in a rounded point in the front. She checked herself and decided the ensemble looked different enough from the last time she wore the dress. She took a deep breath and walked gracefully down the beautiful stairs.

Johnnie checked the bar and rearranged the flowers one more time. Then she went to the kitchen to help get the hors d'oeuvres ready. She tied on a party apron and helped Blanca fill the puff pastries with the chicken mixture. They got the vegetable plate out and filled the red cabbage with the green goddess mayonnaise. She was pleased with the red and green combination. Since it was very close to party time, they carried everything out to the foyer and set it up. Johnnie just couldn't believe how smoothly everything was going.

"Oh, Johnnie, that dress is beautiful on you and your eyes are just so green," Iris said as she entered the foyer.

"You look very nice in your dress too, Mother. Now if you want to join us you know you're certainly welcome."

Her mother was dressed in a pale mauve silk crepe gown that had pearls embroidered on the long sleeves, and she wore a pearl necklace, pin, and earrings.

"No, I'll just eat in the breakfast room. I don't want to interfere with your friends."

"Okay, Mother," Johnnie said. "I do appreciate you greeting them."

Patrick came home that moment.

"Oh, don't you ladies look beautiful? I'll have to hurry because we finished late on the golf course. Lionel disappeared a couple times again," Patrick said as he rushed upstairs.

"They played golf on Friday?" Iris asked, confused.

"Yes, Patrick doesn't have afternoon classes on Friday and the other men can work their own schedules."

Colleen came down the beautiful stairs at that moment as gracefully as her mother. She was dressed in a silk print dress of greens and blues. In her hair, she had fastened a small Christmas pin.

"You look beautiful, Colleen," Johnnie said giving her daughter a squeeze.

"Ladies, you all will be the prettiest by far at the party tonight," Patrick declared as he came downstairs to join them, dressed in a dark navy suit and a red Christmas tie.

"And you will be the most handsome by far," Johnnie whispered to her gorgeous husband.

Twenty-six

Johnnie and Patrick kept busy for the next few minutes greeting their guests, Tom and Lisa Johnston, Carol and George Hampton, and Lionel and friend. There was an awkward moment when Lionel walked in and the women noticed his friend's dress, a burgundy velvet number that looked like it was painted on her full, curvaceous figure. He did not introduce her and she was aloof enough that no one approached her.

Almost everyone raved about the cocktail hour and the hors d'oeuvres, except Lionel who seemed to study the appetizers more than eat them and his usually cordial countenance took on a surly look. "The Babe" stood next to him, sipping her bourbon and soda, not saying a word and looking at no one.

Johnnie barely noticed the couple, instead taking in all the compliments with a pleased smile. *Yes,* she thought, *everything is going well but I had better not be too prideful, pride goeth before a fall.*

When they started dinner with the deviled crab, everyone couldn't say enough good things about the dish except Lionel and his date. Lionel picked at his dish and his countenance took on an even more hostile look, his dark eyes flashing. But Johnnie didn't notice because the others were laughing and talking and having a great time. Dr. Tom always could liven up a party with funny stories from his practice.

Johnnie mixed the salad with drama and served it without a hitch. They had a light Chardonnay with the crab but no wine with the salad. The main course of the beef tenderloin with cipollini onions argodolce was enjoyed quietly as everyone concentrated on the wonderful meal. The guests raved over the imaginative side dishes, which were set off by the Bordeaux that Patrick had chosen. Everyone was busy eating except Lionel, who grew more menacing by the course. It seemed the happier Johnnie got, the crosser Lionel became, but she was too busy basking in all the compliments to notice that the odd couple at the end of the table didn't seem to appreciate the meal as much as the others.

While Blanca cleared the plates, Johnnie got up to get the coffee from the butler's pantry. After the table was clean, Blanca brought out the coconut rum flan and almond crisps. *Blanca sure moves a lot faster than I do,* Johnnie thought.

Johnnie felt air movement even though she could see Blanca in the kitchen. At that moment, she felt a presence next to her. Looking up into Lionel's menacing face, her heart stopped, or so it seemed, and she held her breath.

"Where did you get those recipes?" Lionel said in a low hostile whisper, his face in a cruel grimace.

He was standing too close; she could feel his hot breath when he spoke. His hands were clenched in tight fists and his eyes were shining with malice. *Was he going to punch her right in her own house? Would anyone even notice?* They were all having such a good time in the dining room. She moved away a little in the tight quarters and smiled in her most winning way, hoping to defuse the situation with kindness.

"Linda gave them to me to kitchen test for her and I thought this would be a perfect opportunity. Did you think I prepared everything correctly?" Johnnie answered as sweetly as she could, her voice high and squeaking.

"When did she give you those recipes? She never told me anything about it," he hissed.

"One afternoon shortly before she left. I copied them in my notebook so I could make notes for her. When is she coming back anyway?" Johnnie said still talking in a high squeaking voice.

With that, Lionel stormed out of the room, gathered up "the Babe," and marched out of the house.

126

"Wow, what was that all about?" George asked with awe.

"Must have been something he ate," Barb said.

Johnnie shrugged her shoulders and tried to pass the whole thing off as nothing even though her heart was pounding.

Well, she thought, *pride does goeth before a fall.* She worked hard to enjoy the rest of the evening, especially since everyone else was, but her heart wasn't really in it any more.

"Johnnie, that was a great party even if Lionel didn't stay till the finish," Patrick opined, hugging his wife as their guests left. "Thank you, my sweet."

Twenty-seven

Johnnie rested on the cool cement bench on the landing since the old furniture was carefully stored for the winter. She stared at nothing in particular, trying to replay the awful scene with Lionel one more time. It was the Wednesday after the Golfer's Dinner before she had time to hide away from everybody and think. She shivered even though it was warm and sunny and wrapped her arms around herself.

Why did Lionel have such a strong reaction to the recipes? She never expected such a strong reaction although she wasn't quite sure what she thought he would do. Probably nothing, because certainly Patrick would never notice any thing in particular about a meal she prepared. He was always very appreciative for anything she put in front of him, but he didn't have an idea about how anything was made. She couldn't remember Linda ever mentioning Lionel sharing time in the kitchen, but maybe he was particular.

As she remembered the two parties for Charles, she reconsidered, realizing he probably took a much more active part in the meal planning than Patrick ever did. And the recipe cards she took were labeled Lionel's favorites. What it all meant she just didn't know. She didn't want to discuss this mystery because no one else seemed to be concerned about Linda...and she certainly wasn't going to share what she did with the recipes with Patrick.

"Johnnie, oh Johnnie," her mother called.

"Mother, don't come down the stairs. I'll come up to you," Johnnie answered, not wanting her mother walking down the steep staircase.

Johnnie ran up the stairs to her mother before her mother could start down. Iris wasn't in great health and tired easily; Johnnie didn't think her sight was very good either.

"Johnnie, Blanca and I are going to make dinner tonight if that's all right," Iris said.

"That's fine, Mother. Did you finish your shopping?" Johnnie asked.

"Yes, Colleen took me to Buffin's and then the May Company on the way back from the Santa Anita Mall. I've finished everything now." Iris said.

"Sounds like you had a successful trip!" Johnnie wondered how many of the other family members had finished their Christmas shopping and hoped all of them had.

As Johnnie worked in her office, she could hear her mother and Blanca cooking and smiled to herself. Her mother was telling Blanca her superstition about the onions and instructing her not to keep any leftovers and to throw any of the peelings right out of the house. Johnnie thought that was probably the way her mother had chosen to get the garbage taken out. It had sure worked in her mother's house.

After the lovely dinner of roast beef, scalloped potatoes, green beans almandine, a tossed green salad, and apple pie for dessert, Johnnie retired to the library where she had Patrick build a fire even though it wasn't very cold. She just wanted to stare at the flames for a while.

Patrick came in and sat close to Johnnie.

"Are you feeling okay, Johnnie? Not getting sick so close to Christmas, are you?" Patrick inquired as he cuddled his wife.

"Guess I'm just a little tired, that's all," Johnnie replied, unable to share what was worrying her with her husband.

"Then let's go upstairs. I've got an early meeting tomorrow so might as well go to bed," Patrick said.

Johnnie slept a deep, dead sleep that night.

Twenty-eight

"Christmas 1980 was the best ever," Iris said.

Of course, her mother said that after every Christmas, Johnnie thought with a happy smile. Uncle Pete, acting his usual self, had put more pressure on her mother to move in with her or Aunt Rose. He was almost obnoxious about it. Johnnie wasn't sure how her mother took it, but actually, she would like to have her closer.

But now they needed to get ready for Larry and his family's impending visit. Johnnie had told her mother this morning that they would be picking Larry and the others up at the airport in the late afternoon. Her mother was insisting on coming with them, and Johnnie didn't know what to do about it. It would just have to work out some how.

Larry's visit turned out better than Johnnie could have imagined. Her sister-in-law, Carol, turned out to be a bridge player and the women of the house had a wonderful time playing cards day and night. Johnnie hadn't had someone to play bridge with for a long time.

Her nephews didn't make any trouble, and Colleen and Ian took them all over—Disneyland, Universal Studios, Magic Mountain, and Knots Berry Farm. They even took them down to Newport Beach to watch the surfers.

It's already New Year's Eve and their visit is coming to an end, Johnnie thought with sadness. She didn't realize how much she missed her brother and his family. She took lots of pictures so she could add them to her little gallery on the tall dresser.

"Mom, the boys want to have some Mexican food before they leave," Ian announced as he walked into the breakfast room where

130

Johnnie was sipping coffee and reading the paper.

"Take them to Ernie Taco Juniors up on Colorado Street. That should do it for them," Johnnie said, passing some more money to her younger son.

When she was finished with the Arts section, she checked her watch and realized some time had passed since she spoke with Ian. In fact, the kids had gone to the restaurant, eaten, and come back. She needed to go get ready for the evening's festivities. She and Patrick were going to the Country Club for the New Year's dinner and dance, with Carol and Larry as their guests. The others were going to be having a wonderful dinner at home and her nephews would be spending the evening at home with their grandmother. Colleen and Ian both had plans.

As Johnnie and Patrick got dressed, sipping a private glass of champagne, they talked about 1980, going over the missed Olympics, the failed rescue of the Iran hostages, the eruption of Mt. St. Helens and Harry Truman who died in the eruption, their new president, President Reagan, and the murder of the former Beatle John Lennon. As they talked, Johnnie wondered if she could be like Harry Truman, the man, not the President, and stand up for what she believed in even if it meant her death. *Well, Linda, I am going to find out what happened to you and hopefully it won't mean my death.* With that thought, she finished dressing in her ball gown of silvery blue silk brocade. It had a fitted bodice enhanced by a low cut neckline with silver-threaded straps over her shoulders. The skirt billowed out gracefully from the waistline and was perfect for all the dancing she planned to do.

But checking herself in the mirror, she noticed the dress was just hanging on her. *Guess it's all the swimming,* she thought as she carefully took the dress off and returned it to the closet. *Now what can I wear?* She pulled the green cocktail dress out of her closet and decided it would do; she knew it fit okay and she could cinch it in with the rhinestone belt that came with it. She decided to wear her very best jewelry, a matched set of necklace and earrings in platinum and diamonds.

After some reflection, Johnnie decided against the matching pin. Patrick might find it uncomfortable when they danced and she didn't want anything to interrupt their dancing. Holding her pin, she decided to fasten it in her hair like Colleen had done for the golfer's Christmas party. She fixed her hair in a tight twist and fastened the clip against the inside of the twist toward the top. Then she took the beautiful platinum band with diamonds and sapphires, the ring that Patrick had surprised her with on Christmas, and put it on her right hand on her ring finger. She looked lovingly at the ring, happy that she had a husband who would give her such a beautiful present. She wore strappy silver high-heeled sandals. Patrick wore the tuxedo that Johnnie always liked on him.

"Don't we just make a striking couple," Johnnie murmured, taking her husband's arm.

Patrick leaned over kissed his wife and softly hugged her. "Johnnie, thank you for being there for me all these years. Here's to many more." Johnnie accepted the glass he handed her and joined him in the toast. They all had a spectacular time at the country club. The food was outstanding; it began with a clear soup, then the salad, followed by roast beef, mushroom-shaped potatoes, and a vegetable medley with lemon sauce. The wines were matched with each course except the salad. There was a dessert carousel in another room where they could choose just about any kind of sweet concoction they wanted.

The band was wonderful and Johnnie danced many dances with Patrick and some with Larry. Barb and Stan were at the table with them, but Stan really didn't like to dance so they just watched, seeming to enjoy themselves.

"Johnnie, did you see Lionel and friend out on the dance floor? Her dress couldn't be any tighter or lower cut. They make some kind of couple out there," Barb gossiped.

"No, I didn't see them. Are they out there now? Can you show me inconspicuously where they are?" Johnnie leaned over and whispered back.

"If you look toward the band and to the left, you may have to stand up, you will see the 'lovely couple.' Do you think we should send one of the guys over to wherever they are sitting to wish them a happy New Year? Maybe I can get Stan to do it," Barb said to Johnnie quietly.

"If Stan would be willing it would be interesting to know who they are sitting with since Linda always sat with us. And maybe he could get an introduction to 'the Babe,' " Johnnie said.

Stan, willing, went to find Lionel and friend but couldn't find them on the dance floor, or anywhere else in the building after making a thorough search.

"Couldn't find them anywhere, honey," Stan said when he returned from his tour.

"If you couldn't find them then they aren't here, Stan, you're good at finding people. Thanks for looking, anyway," Barb said, giving Stan a quick kiss.

They all toasted the New Year at midnight with lots of hugs and kisses. Then back at their home in their own bedroom with the door closed Johnnie and Patrick had their own spectacular time welcoming in 1981.

January

…one has to court doubt and darkness as the cost of knowing…

Four Things, H. Van Dyke 1920

Twenty-nine

Johnnie woke early on January first feeling fresh, invigorated, and ready to face the New Year head on. She showered quickly, knowing her mother likes to get up early and watch the pre-parade show, and her children were taking Larry, Carol, and the nephews to the Rose Parade. They planned to sit in the bleachers instead of going to George Hampton's office—it was upstairs and on the parade route and he always offered it to people who wanted a good seat without the hassle of the crowds. They usually accepted, but Johnnie didn't want to impose on George with five more people. Instead, they'd packed an extensive picnic basket to snack on.

She hummed happily as she dressed in a wool Pendleton pants in a plaid of reds and blues. She wore a loosely fitted white fuzzy sweater with a cowl neckline, pulled her hair back at her neck with a tortoise shell clip, and slipped into her navy moccasins. As the final touch, she added small gold knots for earrings. She skipped down the beautiful stairs and waltzed into the kitchen to start the coffee.

"Oh, Blanca, I didn't expect you today, after all, it's a holiday. Happy New Year," Johnnie greeted Blanca cheerfully when she found the housekeeper busy in the kitchen.

"Mrs. Collins, I am making a good breakfast because we all must start the new year right," Blanca said seriously.

"Okay! It sure smells good. I'll get whoever I can up," Johnnie said.

Most everyone in the house did manage to get up to eat the wonderful breakfast Blanca made with blueberry muffins, apple spice muffins, a fruit salad, bacon, a frittata, and hot cereal with raisins and dates.

After breakfast there was a flurry getting those who were going to the parade off. After they got everybody sorted out into cars, Johnnie made sure Iris and Aunt Rose were settled in to watch the parade on the big screen TV in the family room. *It just seems to take so much time to get everyone ready to go anywhere*, Johnnie thought to herself, trying not to get aggravated on New Year's Day. *Oh well, at least when they get home the next round won't be so difficult, it's just Larry and Patrick!*

This year the men got tickets for the game because Larry was in town. Johnnie didn't ask how much the tickets cost or how they did it since not one of them went to either of the colleges, Washington or Michigan.

"Did I miss breakfast?" Patrick asked, coming down into the foyer where Johnnie was standing after the parade-goers finally left.

He gave his wife a big kiss and squeezy hug.

"Happy New Year, my sweet. Thanks for last night, we sure welcomed in 1981. How about breakfast? I'm famished." Patrick said softly in Johnnie's ear.

"Mmm, let's see if there's anything left. Blanca doesn't want us starting the new year without a good breakfast," Johnnie said pulling away from Patrick, taking his hand and leading him into the breakfast room.

"Mr. Collins, I've saved some muffins for you," Blanca said on seeing Patrick.

"Everything looks great and smells good too, Blanca. Bring it on, I didn't know I was so hungry," Patrick said.

Blanca made sure everyone, including Aunt Rose, had a good breakfast before she left to go spend the day with Henry.

Johnnie, her mom, and Aunt Rose spent the morning enjoying the Rose Parade.

"Another beautiful parade. Didn't Lorne Greene make a nice Grand Marshall and wasn't Leslie Kawai just a beautiful Rose Queen?" As the parade finished, Iris had just one complaint; "I just wish they wouldn't rush everything so trying to get finished for all those football games."

"Yes, there are a number of bowl games nowadays," Rose said as they all left the room.

Johnnie and her mother fixed a buffet of ham, roast beef, potato salad, the cole slaw they made the day before, fresh baked rolls, baked beans, and a relish tray. Blanca had made a lovely chocolate cake for the buffet before she left for her own quarters. They would have the spread out for anyone to munch on whenever. Aunt Rose kept them company in the kitchen as they worked.

"Johnnie and Iris, I might as well tell you now. I'm not going to retire completely this January. Too much is going on but I will take more time off. Guess everyone but me knew I wouldn't retire," Rose said with irony.

"Aunt Rose, you have to do what you're comfortable doing," Johnnie said, wrapping her a tight embrace.

The parade-goers came back starved even though they had eaten everything in the picnic basket; Johnnie was glad they had the buffet set up already. Later, the men took off for the Rose Bowl game. Over dinner that night, she got a full run-down on the experience from her brother.

"It was a great game, especially since we could root for whichever team was winning! Not going to the schools that were invited was a hidden bonus, I suppose," Patrick said.

"The Huskies had more total yards against the Wolverines but it wasn't enough for them to win. This was the Wolverines' first Rose Bowl win in six tries, so good for them. Don Bracken's seventy-three-yard punt in the first quarter set a Rose Bowl record," Larry said. "And I'm so happy we got to go in person to the parade and then the game. Thank you, Patrick and Johnnie. We've had just a wonderful vacation, rain and all. I'm just glad today was clear and sunny."

Thirty

Johnnie sat chatting with her mother in the breakfast room, drinking coffee and trying to ease the quiet of the now-empty house.

"Wow, I didn't think they would make their plane. I don't know why it takes everyone so long to get ready," Johnnie complained. "Good thing we got them up nice and early this morning, although I don't think any of them appreciated it. Wasn't it just so wonderful to have Larry and family here this last week? And it was good to get to know Carol better, don't you think, Mother?"

"Oh, I just hated to see them go, even though I know they have their own lives and we wouldn't have it any other way," Iris replied, fighting back tears.

Johnnie reached over, took her mother's hand and gave it a soft squeeze. It had been hard to say goodbye. They didn't go to the airport with the others because Johnnie knew that her mother wouldn't be able to make the trip. Aunt Rose came over early, before they left, to say goodbye. Uncle Pete called them early before they left. It was sad to see them go and Johnnie worked hard not to join her mother in tears.

"What's got my two ladies so blue?" Patrick asked as he walked into the room and kissed Johnnie on the forehead.

"We're just missing Larry and family, that's all," Johnnie said, sighing.

"Well, let me finish the morning for you. Lionel wants us to help him with another one of his meetings this coming Saturday morning. It will be in a hotel conference room. I told him we would help. Sorry," Patrick said.

"Oh, Patrick, you didn't. I don't want to do any more of those parties," Johnnie said with a whine in her voice that she didn't like. "He just wants us to greet the people because he has an appointment he can't break. He'll join us just as soon as he can get away, then we can leave. I just couldn't get a word in to tell him no. I'm really sorry," Patrick apologized again.

"Oh it's all right, I'm just a little tired today," Johnnie replied, rubbing her shoulder against Patrick's.

"Since we still have a holiday because the first was Thursday, I think I'll see if I can't get a golf game together."

"Guess I'll go swim some. I have to keep working for the meet," Johnnie said.

"Rose wants me to do some things with her today. This will work out just right with all of us taking off," Iris said.

Once Johnnie got to the country club, she swam many laps, a little surprised at how much she enjoyed the exercise. She was glad she told Coach Hank she would be on the team. Not only was he having her swim lots of laps, but he wanted her working out on the Solo Flex. She really was becoming a much stronger swimmer.

As she walked out of the country club, she heard Barb call her and was happy to stop.

"Barb, it's good to see you!" Johnnie said.

"Do you have time for a cocktail?" Barb asked.

"Sure, everyone at home is busy doing something," Johnnie said.

The ladies settled themselves in a booth after they got to the bar. Johnnie ordered a glass of Chardonnay and Barb, Scotch and water.

"Barb, Lionel wants us to help with another one of those blasted parties and Patrick told him we would. Even worse, I couldn't really get angry with Patrick because I know Lionel can be overbearing sometimes," Johnnie said.

"You mean a party with Charles?" Barb asked with a little too much enthusiasm.

"Yes, a party with Charles at the Biltmore in downtown Los Angeles. I'm really not looking forward to it at all. The party is this Saturday morning and we probably won't know anyone again," Johnnie said with resentment.

"Johnnie, why don't you tell Patrick you just don't want to do it?" Barb asked.

"I should but somehow I can't. He was so sorry about getting us into the mess; I don't have the heart to make him get us out of it," Johnnie said.

"That's just why Lionel keeps getting you to help him. Neither one of you can say no," Barb said.

"You're right, Barb, of course. But maybe I can find out when Linda is coming back," Johnnie said.

"Okay, but don't count on finding anything out from Lionel. Stan said that George Hampton tried several times with unpleasant results and no answer," Barb said.

The ladies talked about the New Year's Eve party and the visit of Larry and family and the visit of Barb's daughter home on leave from the Navy. Johnnie enjoyed Barb's company and they laughed and talked through several rounds of their drinks. They decided to order lunch and continue their visit so it was mid afternoon when Johnnie finally left the country club.

Thirty-one

Johnnie woke from a restless sleep with a sense of dread Saturday morning. She really didn't want to go to downtown Los Angeles to host another business meeting disguised as a party. She rolled out of bed slowly and walked listlessly past the tall chest on the way into the dressing area and bathroom. She stopped for a moment to gaze at her children's pictures and sighed. Some mornings even the kids weren't enough to cheer her up.

After showering, she decided to dress in formal business clothes. She chose a beige wool suit and a light blue silk blouse with ruffles going down the v cut of the blouse. She drew her hair back at the sides with tortoise shell clips, slipped in small, gold doorknocker-style earrings, and decided to ask Patrick for help with the clasp of her choker necklace. Then she added a pair of sturdy brown leather pumps and a matching purse. After studying her appearance in the full-length mirror, she decided she looked okay even though the waist-band of the skirt was a lot looser than it used to be. *Must be all that swimming,* she thought.

"Patrick, time to get up. We have a meeting to go to," Johnnie said in Patrick's ear softly.

"Huh? Oh, okay. I'm getting up," Patrick said working to wake himself up.

At least he got some sleep, Johnnie thought to herself. *He'll need to be rested to drive over that Pasadena Freeway.* Johnnie didn't like the old freeway, it had small lanes, lots of curves, and no lane to turn off on for emergencies. If she had her way, they would go over Huntington Drive to get downtown, but since Patrick didn't seem to mind the Pasadena Freeway, she would just close her eyes till they got to the Hill Street off-ramp. She loved to see the city from that view and the weather was clear and crisp so the city wouldn't be covered with smog.

The drive downtown wasn't too bad. The freeway wasn't crowded since it was Saturday but that also meant that everyone drove faster. Johnnie tried to concentrate on what they were to do once they were in the hotel. Lionel had given them a list of the people who planned to attend and they were to cross off the names when the people arrived. That meant they would need to ask everyone their name; Johnnie sighed and marveled again how her usually wonderful husband got them roped into this.

Fortunately, the view of Los Angeles as they came around a curve and up the hill gave Johnnie a lift. She sat up straighter as she saw the tall, dark Arco Towers thinking how for years no one was allowed to build tall buildings because of earthquakes.

They found a parking lot across the street from the Biltmore; it was going to cost a king's ransom, but they had come prepared. Johnnie was just glad they didn't have to park in Pershing Square and walk back. Even though the parking lot was really just an old weed-infested black top with a chain link fence around it, there was a man taking the tickets so at least someone would be watching their car.

Inside the hotel, they fumbled a little finding the room Lionel reserved and felt like country kids come to the big city. They sure hoped the guests wouldn't have as much trouble.

"I see the coffee and rolls were delivered," Patrick said, helping himself to a cup of coffee.

"I think if we set ourselves up here we'll be able to catch everyone as they come in. I wonder where Charles is? He really should be here by now," Johnnie said.

People started coming in and Patrick and Johnnie were kept busy getting the names crossed off. They directed the people over the to the coffee and rolls, not knowing what else to do. Charles Defoe was still not there and Lionel was not expected until later. Johnnie and Patrick looked at each other when the last name was crossed off and wondered what to do next. Just then another guest walked up, a man

146

in a brown suit with a grim look. They already had the list of names completely crossed off, so who was this? Johnnie began to think she'd never get out of this event.

"Is this the investment meeting being hosted by Charles Defoe?"

"Yes," Johnnie replied. Her heart started to beat a little harder as she realized something was wrong.

"Something we can help you with?" Patrick asked firmly.

"Yes, I'm Lieutenant Olsen and I want to talk with Charles Defoe, but in the meantime if you will have all these people take a seat I want to make an announcement," Lieutenant Olsen said as he pulled out his wallet and showed his identification.

"Okay, Johnnie, let's get everyone to sit down," Patrick agreed.

They both moved quickly into the room and quietly asked the people to find a chair. Once everyone was seated they took a seat too. If the lieutenant wanted to take over the meeting, he could do just that as far as they were concerned.

Johnnie fiddled with her rings and squirmed in her seat. *Where was Charles and why couldn't Lionel just get here?* Her heart was beating wildly. Patrick took her hand and smiled weakly at her.

"Ladies and gentleman, I'm Lieutenant Olsen from the Los Angeles Police Department. You've just been saved from making a terrible investment. I want you all to go home now and be glad you still have your money."

With that everyone got up to leave, murmuring to each other. Johnnie and Patrick sat in shock and didn't get up right away.

"You two stay, I want to talk to you," Lieutenant Olsen said.

"Yes, sir, we'll wait," Patrick said.

Johnnie felt miserable. *What did the lieutenant want from them? They knew nothing. Had they made a bad investment?* This day was not turning out well, and they were so far from home, with strangers.

"So, what can you tell me about Charles Defoe?" Lieutenant Olsen started once the room was clear.

"We're investors with his company," Patrick answered.

"Well, you people have been part of a pyramid scheme and I'm afraid you lost whatever money you invested. We've been after Mr.

Defoe, and that is an alias, for a long time.

They talked with the lieutenant for a little while longer before he said they could leave. They walked silently out of the hotel, crossed the street, got their car, paid for the parking, and got back on the Pasadena Freeway. Johnnie didn't even notice the ride she was so deep in thought.

"Johnnie, do you still have the business card Charles gave you?" Patrick said.

"Yes, he has an office on Lake Street near Bullocks."

"Then that's where we are going next," Patrick said.

They past their off ramp for Orange Grove and instead they continued to the end of the freeway and drove up to Del Mar making a left on Lake Street. On Lake Street they drove past the building where Charles had his office while trying to find a parking place. There was a For Lease sign posted. Now Johnnie really felt sick. *Was this the office Charles had or some other office? Guess we'll know soon enough*, she thought with dread.

After they finally found a parking place, they walked quickly to the office building. They wrote the phone number down off the lease sign, found a pay phone in Bullock's, and called the number. They arranged to have the real estate representative give them a tour of the available office space. Sadly, the office that had been so tastefully decorated, the office that made Charles Defoe look so successful, the one that Barb and Johnnie visited was the empty office being leased.

"Oh, Patrick, everyone lost their money, even our neighbors. This is just awful," Johnnie cried as they walked back to their car.

Patrick put his arm around Johnnie and gave her a squeeze. "We all knew there was a risk. I just would have been happier to lose my money on a bad investment instead of feathering someone's nest."

When they finally got home, they both came into the house so droopy it was obvious to everyone that something was wrong.

"What's wrong, Mother?" Colleen looked concerned.

"Is everything all right?" Iris asked upon seeing the couple.

"Oh, it's nothing life threatening just very disappointing. Our investment with Charles Defoe turned out to be part of a pyramid scheme, unfortunately," Johnnie replied.

"Oh, honey, I'm just so sorry," Iris said, giving her daughter a big hug.

Iris then headed for the kitchen. Patrick went to his study and Johnnie headed upstairs to work out a little. She walked by the tall dresser on the way into the dressing room to change into work out clothes. She stopped at the pictures of her children and studied them for a while before moving on.

She did the work out on the Solo Flex machine that she and coach Hank had set for her. She was now up a notch on the "rubber bands" and was proud of her achievement. She found the Solo Flex a much easier way to do weight training, although the actual exercise was a good work out.

After working out, she went back to her bedroom and then decided to take a relaxing bubble bath. She tried to relax, but her mind just kept working on the betrayal. *Did the great Lionel Marshall have a part in it? How would the neighbors take the news?* She sighed and guessed she'd find out soon enough.

She decided to wear her winter white cashmere pants outfit. She chose a pink quartz necklace and earring set and a chunky gold bracelet, accented with icy pink lipstick and a pink blush. Her shoes for the evening were high heeled peau de soie pumps. She dabbed some Red Door cologne behind both ears, and fixed her hair in an upsweep. She checked herself and sighed.

Johnnie walked slowly down the beautiful staircase, grateful they hadn't used the house as collateral for their bad investment.

"You look so beautiful, my sweet," Patrick said coming up to her and kissing her with passion.

"Oh, Patrick," Johnnie moaned, kissing him back.

"Come on, let's go into the living room. Your mother has been busy."

"Yes, she likes to cook whenever there is trouble. So, we probably are in for a treat tonight. I just hope I can eat what she's prepared," Johnnie said.

Iris and Blanca had been busy in the kitchen. Blanca prepared some canapés of cherry tomato and avocado, and crab salad for the cocktail hour. She also put out a bowl of mixed nuts from See's Candy.

"What can I fix for you this evening, Mrs. Collins," Patrick said, standing at the cart with the cocktail fixings.

"Tonight I would like a martini, Mr. Collins."

Patrick fixed two martinis and they settled on the sofa side by side, sipping their drinks, nibbling on the canapés, and watching the sun set from the bay window. They were both lost in thought when the doorbell rung.

"Mr. and Mrs. Collins, it's Mr. Marshall to see you," Blanca announced.

Patrick rose from the sofa and walked out into the foyer. Johnnie wondered what this was all about but did not want to greet Lionel or "the Babe."

"Good evening, Mrs. Collins," Lionel said, strolling into the living room with Patrick following.

"Good evening, Lionel," Johnnie said from the sofa not wanting to get any closer to Lionel and checking quickly behind him to see if "the Babe" was with him. She wasn't.

"Join us for cocktails," Patrick offered.

Johnnie's heart sank. She really didn't want to entertain anyone right now, especially Lionel.

"Thank you, I'll have whatever you're drinking," Lionel said as he collapsed into an easy chair close to the sofa.

Johnnie wanted to move, Lionel was just too close; his feet were almost touching hers. She made a mental note to move that chair further from the sofa the next chance she got.

"Umm these appetizers are just delicious," Lionel said piling his plate high.

"So, did you hear what happened to us downtown this morning, Lionel?" Johnnie inquired.

"Yes, Lieutenant Olsen got in touch with me too. I just don't know what to do. All my friends and neighbors made investments with this skunk. I just don't know what to do," Lionel repeated.

Well, he certainly seems sorry, Johnnie thought to herself. *Maybe he's a good actor.*

It was getting close to the dinner hour and Lionel wasn't moving from his chair.

"Will you join us for dinner this evening, Lionel?" Patrick said.

When Johnnie saw that they were having chicken Kiev, she wondered who would have to eat something else since usually there wasn't extra. Colleen and her mother both ate in the breakfast room. *Probably to cover up the different dinner,* Johnnie thought bitterly.

Over dinner, Lionel told them more details about the skunk named Charles Defoe. Apparently the furniture in the office was leased for just six months, as was the office. The luxury car he drove was rented for short periods off and on. He'd run up charge bills all over town and made no effort to pay any of them. He was truly a skunk.

"How did you meet Charles or whatever his name is?"

"I was introduced to him at a party and he was given great references," Lionel said.

Johnnie almost felt sorry for Lionel. He looked old, tired, and dejected. *Too bad he doesn't have Linda to help him through this.*

"I'm going to have all the neighbors who invested over and have Paul Graham, you met him at the second party, he's a defense lawyer, talk with them. I don't want any of them suing me," Lionel said when the dinner was almost over.

"That's a good idea Lionel," Patrick said. "And we'll be there for support."

Oh bother, Johnnie thought. *I don't want to face the neighbors in their misery and mine.*

"Great then; I'll get it set up for this next week," Lionel said. "The sooner the better."

Thirty-two

Monday, Johnnie rose early and got to the country club even before they were finished opening so she could swim her laps before going to work. She wanted to avoid running into Barb until the news was out about Charles Defoe.

She kept busy at work helping the group that was working on the plan presented by Bill Stern. The group was not looking at the numbers as optimistically as Bill had and Johnnie wondered if there would be another loud meeting with Mr. Stern. Not something she looked forward to at all.

Arriving home after Patrick, she really appreciated that Blanca was there to make dinner. She did regret having spent so much time away from home when Colleen would be leaving soon. But then, Colleen never stayed around the house anyway.

"Everything smells wonderful, Blanca," Johnnie said coming in through the kitchen.

"Oh thank you, Mrs. Collins," Blanca replied, blushing. "Mr. Collins said for you to join him in the living room when you got home."

Johnnie walked toward the living room wondering what Patrick wanted so vitally that she couldn't go change her clothes first.

"Patrick, darling, I'm home at last," Johnnie teased.

Patrick was sitting on the sofa holding an envelope with the rest of the mail sitting on the side table.

"Lionel didn't waste much time getting the meeting set up," Patrick said as Johnnie took a seat next to him.

Handing the envelope to his wife, he gave her a nice hello kiss.

"I think he walked these invitations around the neighborhood.

152

There's no stamp on the envelope," Johnnie said..

"Yes, he must have done that after he left last night," Patrick said. Johnnie took the letter out of the envelope. It simply said that Lionel wanted to meet with the investors and had arranged for a meeting room in the Pasadena Hilton for Wednesday night at seven o'clock.

"Well, we'll have to have an early dinner Wednesday," Johnnie said.

"We better come up with some story if any of the investors asked us what this is about. George and Tom knew we were going to that Saturday meeting. Or we better keep out of sight," Patrick said.

"I think we'll do better keeping out of sight. At least you don't work with Tom or George and you won't be playing golf until after the meeting," Johnnie said.

"We might not be playing golf as a foursome at all after this meeting," Patrick said.

"Oh, Patrick, you don't think this will mean we'll lose our friendships?" Johnnie asked.

"We just don't know how some of the others will feel about losing their investment. We were careful not to use money we needed right away. Although it's not great to have lost our money, it won't put us in the poor house," Patrick said.

That was something Johnnie hadn't thought about. *People could be funny about their money,* she realized with dread. Now she really didn't want to go to the meeting at all but knew she had to so people wouldn't wonder where they were.

The rest of the evening passed somehow, but she hardly noticed. Colleen would be leaving early the next day so she had gone to bed shortly after dinner. Her mother followed almost immediately.

Johnnie decided to work out on the Solo Flex before she called the evening done. The workout helped clear her head and made her feel a little more positive. With only two days to worry about, she knew she and Patrick could keep out of sight. Sometimes she went for a week without seeing any neighbors. That night she slept peacefully snuggled next to Patrick.

Tuesday passed in a blur. Colleen left early; Johnnie swam early and drove straight to work, staying until after dark before driving home. She was glad Blanca was there to keep her mother company.

Wednesday, Johnnie woke with dread.

"Don't forget to come home early, Patrick. We have *the meeting* tonight," Johnnie reminded him over a quick breakfast.

"No, I haven't forgotten. One more day to hide out," Patrick said kissing Johnnie as he left for work.

Johnnie decided to stay home with her mother and maybe they would do something. They could drive out to Arcadia and visit Uncle Pete. That would keep her out of sight for a while, at least.

Uncle Pete was delighted to have the ladies for the afternoon. They went to Peppers for lunch because Uncle Pete just had a taste for some Mexican food. They laughed and talked the hours away.

"Wasn't that such a nice visit? Thanks for taking me, Johnnie," Iris said once they were back home.

"Yes, I enjoyed it too, Mother," Johnnie said.

Johnnie wondered how her mother felt about the pressure Uncle Pete continued to put on her to move in with Johnnie or Aunt Rose. But Iris didn't seem to notice or maybe she was making it a point not to notice.

She left her mother downstairs with Blanca, went up the back stairs to her bedroom stopping at the pictures of her children and admired the new school photos of her nephews, which were held in a special frame. That way the little photos didn't look too out of place with the portraits. She stared at the children for a while then continued into the bathroom.

She showered quickly and dressed in a navy blue wool crepe dress with long sleeves, belted waist, and tulip-shaped skirt. The dress had a collar and buttons down to the waist. In the open neckline, she wore a simple strand of pearls and then added matching pearl earrings. It was getting harder to find clothes in her closet that fit. With all the swimming and the workouts on the Solo Flex, her figure was changing. She wondered if she would have to replace her wardrobe. *What a thing to be thinking about this evening,* she thought.

"A penny for your thoughts," Patrick offered.

"They're not worth a penny," Johnnie laughed.

"You look just perfect for the meeting tonight." Patrick sneaked up on his wife to give her a squeeze and a kiss.

"I just hope everything will go okay," Johnnie said.

"We'll find out soon enough. Let's see what your mother and Blanca made for dinner tonight. By the way, we can celebrate a little because we weren't caught by any of the neighbors. So smile, we aren't in as much trouble as we could be," Patrick said.

Oh, if only that could be true, Johnnie thought as she put a bright, hopeful smile on her face. Patrick took her arm and they walked arm in arm down the beautiful staircase.

Thirty-three

Johnny could hardly finish the delicious dinner her mother had prepared of sweet and sour baked chicken, steamed rice, stir fried vegetables, a hot and spicy watercress and romaine salad, and a pineapple upside down cake for dessert. Johnnie knew her mother was upset and cooking again but just couldn't do justice to the meal. Patrick decided they would go easy on the wine since they were going to the meeting and they only had a glass of Chardonnay with the main dish.

"That was a great dinner, Iris, but now we have to run. Johnnie, let's go," Patrick said as he rose from the table.

Johnnie's stomach churned and her hands were moist. She quickly dried her hands on her napkin and hoped they would stay dry. "Yes, I guess it's time to go. Your dinner was wonderful, Mother, thank you."

They drove up to Los Robles and the Hilton in silence as Johnnie played with her rings and Patrick grimly stared out at the road.

They found the room Lionel had reserved without much trouble and took seats in the back. If they could have sat in the hallway Johnnie would have liked it better. The neighbors who had made investments were talking and laughing amongst themselves. Johnnie felt sick seeing them, knowing they were going to get some very bad news in a few minutes. Her hands were moist again and she fiddled frantically with her rings. Patrick reached over, took her clammy hand and held it. Johnnie cringed inside, knowing her hands were cool and wet, but dear sweet Patrick didn't seem to notice. She wanted to lean over and kiss him.

"Oh boy, here come Lionel and Paul Graham," Patrick whispered.

Lionel was dressed in a finely tailored dark suit, white shirt, and conservative tie, probably silk. Paul Graham looked a little better than the first time Johnnie met him at the second investment party. His brown suit was crisper and he looked fresh—like he just stepped out of the shower. Both men looked so serious it quieted the room. Lionel didn't greet anyone, just nodded to those who tried to say hello. He made his way to the front of the room as Paul Graham followed. *He looks like a puppy,* Johnnie thought. That almost made her laugh and she was afraid if she started, she wouldn't be able to stop.

"Ladies and gentlemen, I invited you here to discuss our investments. Paul Graham is with me and is an investor just as we all are. He is my colleague and also a lawyer. I am turning the meeting over to him now," Lionel said in good loud voice.

Johnnie squirmed in her seat and held her breath while Patrick sat up even straighter than he had been.

"Thank you, Lionel. Ladies and gentlemen, I'm sorry to inform you that Charles Defoe has disappeared, as have our investments. Apparently, Charles Defoe was not his real name and the police have been after him for some time. This is unhappy news for all of us. Lionel will be issuing an official letter to all of you with the details."

There it is, Johnnie thought. The room was very quiet but only for a few seconds before the outcry from the outraged neighbors. It was uglier than Johnnie could ever have imagined. Her neighbors and friends were saying awful things to Paul Graham since Lionel had disappeared. Then they turned on Johnnie and Patrick. Seems they were being held responsible too, since the neighbors thought they were co-hosting with Lionel. Johnnie felt sick and angry with Lionel for putting them in this predicament. George Hampton did try defend them, saying that the Collinses didn't have any more to do with Charles Defoe than the rest of them, but no one would listen. Even sweet Anna Malloy made some remarks against Johnnie and that hurt most of all. She had to fight back tears.

"Patrick, please take me home," Johnnie murmured.

"Yes, let's get out of here," Patrick said.

They drove home in silence, Johnnie trying hard not to cry and Patrick staring intently out the window as he drove. Finally home, they walked hand in hand back into the house, Johnnie hoping her mother hadn't waited up for them because then she would cry. Her own neighbors blaming them for their loss. It was just so unfair.

When they got into their home, Johnnie was relieved that her mother wasn't up. Patrick decided they should have a nightcap to help them relax and poured each of them a glass of sherry.

"That was some meeting. Didn't know our neighbors could be so vicious," Johnnie said as she sipped her sherry.

"Oh, most of them will get over it, but there will be at least one who will always think Lionel and we had something to do with the loss of their money," Patrick replied as he tucked his arm around Johnnie and hugged her.

That night they slept in each other arms, holding each other against the world.

Thirty-four

The Thursday morning after the awful investor's meeting, Johnnie got up not long after Patrick left. She stretched and yawned as she walked past the tall dresser with her pictures, waving to the kids as she walked into the dressing area and bathroom. While showering, she decided she would give all five bathrooms a good, thorough cleaning. It was true that her mother liked to cook when there was trouble, but Johnnie liked to clean under those circumstances. *If we have much more trouble, I won't need Pearl anymore,* she chuckled, trying to cheer herself up.

She dressed in brown corduroy jeans with a dark green turtleneck, and tied her hair in a scarf. Then she went down the back stairs to the breakfast room where her mother was reading recipe books.

"Good morning, Mother. So, what are you finding in the recipe books?" Johnnie asked.

"Just thinking about what to do for dinner tonight. Blanca will be here to help me and I just might want to try something new. Are you going to be cleaning something?" Iris asked.

"Yes, I'm going to give the bathrooms a good scrubbing. You don't have to cook dinner, you know," Johnnie said.

"I know but it gives me pleasure to cook for you and Patrick. The one thing I miss living alone is cooking dinner for a family," Iris said.

After finishing a quick breakfast, Johnnie gathered her cleaning equipment from the utility room off the kitchen. She cleaned the bathrooms on the ground floor first, scrubbing them as if they were very dirty when in fact the rooms were already clean. Blanca and Pearl kept the house sparkling, but Johnnie didn't care, she was driven.

She finished the last bathtub around noon and knew she couldn't move on to the kitchen because her mother would be there working out her own distress. She decided to eat a good lunch because she had worked up an appetite with all the cleaning.

"Mom, do you want some lunch?" Johnnie interrupted once she stored the cleaning equipment.

"Oh, Johnnie! Yes, I need a break," Iris said.

Johnnie wondered what her mother was plotting in the kitchen but she would find out soon enough. The ladies made a lunch of tomato soup and toasted cheese sandwiches that made Johnnie think of her childhood.

After lunch, Johnnie wandered down to her landing and sat on the cold stone bench. She folded her arms around herself and shivered; it was cool sitting on the bench even though the sun was shining. She looked at the yard and was pleased with the work Henry was doing. *The yard is starting to have some grace and style, finally*, she thought. That was the last happy thought she had.

Johnnie just couldn't get the meeting out of her mind and all the hurtful things that were said. *How could anyone think that Lionel or Johnnie or Patrick wanted to have people lose their money? How could the neighbors think that she and Patrick had anything to do with their loss?* No, it just wasn't right and it hurt. And Anna Malloy, kind, sweet Anna Malloy, had joined the ones making accusations and that hurt especially. *How can we ever enjoy ourselves in this neighborhood again? I love this house and the neighborhood and now it's all ruined.* Johnnie started to cry, silently except for the sniffs. She checked her pocket for a tissue and found only one.

It was just so unfair. She could hear Barb saying, "Who told you life is fair, Johnnie?" *I have to stop this and cheer up, so think about good things from the meeting,* she ordered herself. It wasn't all bad, she realized as she reconsidered the previous evening. George Hampton had stood up for them even though his loss was especially painful; he'd refinanced his house and lost his Prop thirteen tax advantage just to get a mortgage with a much higher interest. And Bill Carmichael, gruff Bill the steam-cleaning king, agreed with

George and his wife, Betty, did too. *No, the meeting wasn't all bad,* Johnnie thought as tears streamed down her face.

"Johnnie, Johnnie pull yourself together."

Johnnie felt an arm around her shoulders. Looking up through her tears she saw her mother sitting next to her on the bench. *How did she make it down the stairs,* Johnnie thought in a panic.

"Johnnie, you can't let Patrick see you like this. He already feels bad about how you were treated last night. He's worried about you," Iris said.

"You're right, Mother. Now let's get you back upstairs and see what's happening in the kitchen," Johnnie said.

Johnnie practically had to carry her mother up the stairs from the landing and was glad for all the workouts on the Solo Flex. As they reached the top, she stopped for a moment to catch her breath. She would explain to her mother that there was an intercom on the landing so that she could contact the landing from the house. Maybe that would keep her from walking down the stairs again.

In the house, Johnnie excused herself to take a relaxing bubble bath and get dressed in a pretty outfit. *Guess I am my mother's daughter,* she thought and it made her smile.

After bathing, she put on a billowy outfit in blues and reds on a white background. She twisted her hair up and fastened it with a sparkly comb.

She decided to wear dangling earrings and a sparkly necklace. She slid on the sapphire ring that Patrick gave her for Christmas and looked at it lovingly, stroking it with her left hand. She knew she was blessed to have such a fine man for a husband and three beautiful children. She sighed a long, releasing sigh. Then she put on high navy blue heels with a sparkle accent on the back of the heel. She put a dab of Joy on behind each ear, checked her appearance, and decided she would do.

She walked gracefully down the beautiful staircase, holding herself straight and tall. No one was going to force them out of the neighborhood; she knew that now. She had a family who loved her and that was more important than mean neighbors. Besides, they hadn't done anything wrong except make an investment with the wrong individual.

"Oh, you look just beautiful, Johnnie," Iris said.

"Thank you, Mother, and whatever you are cooking smells heavenly," Johnnie said.

At that moment, Patrick entered through the kitchen door, looking a little unsure of himself. Johnnie smiled one of her most brilliant smiles on seeing him. She could see him stand with more confidence and that made her smile more.

"Johnnie, my beautiful Johnnie," Patrick said, grabbing his wife and kissing her.

"Patrick, I've missed you so much today. But aren't you supposed to be working with Stan this evening?" Johnnie asked.

"Not this Thursday, Stan had a dentist appointment late in the afternoon," Patrick said.

"Oh, that's right, you told me. It's just so good to have you home," Johnnie said hugging her husband.

They walked arm in arm down to Patrick's study where he deposited his briefcase. Then he went upstairs to freshen up before the cocktail hour. Johnnie went with him, not wanting him out of her sight. She knew she was clinging but she just couldn't help herself. She stayed with Patrick while he washed up and talked with him about his day at school, carefully avoiding the topic of the meeting.

Downstairs again, they enjoyed their cocktails with some spicy pecans.

"Mother has been busy in the kitchen all day. She wanted to make something different so I don't know what she cooked. Fortunately, everything does smell good," Johnnie said.

"I know Iris loves to cook for us. I'll go see what she made so I can pick out a wine," Patrick said.

Johnnie just loved Patrick for appreciating her mother's efforts. It made her so happy she had to work not to cry again, this time because she was so happy.

Her mother had made a very special dinner. They had a clear soup to start, then crab imperial for the first course. A salad of Bibb lettuce with hearts of palm, cherry tomatoes, and a dressing of herbed mayonnaise with Balsamic vinaigrette followed. The main course was roast pork tenderloin with wild rice dressing and a side dish of tomato pudding. The dessert was an apple pie cooked in a brown paper bag.

"Mom, this dinner was wonderful and different. Thank you," Johnnie said kissing her mother's forehead.

"Yes, Iris, the dinner was just great!" Patrick agreed heartily.

Johnnie felt so much better. She knew they were going to get through this trouble, just like Patrick tried to tell her the night before. Her smile was genuine and she never stopped smiling all night.

Thirty-five

Johnnie found herself milling around the house, sort of unsettled, that Friday after coming home from swimming her laps. She decided to enjoy a cup of coffee in the living room and stare out the bay window to see if she could settle down. If she couldn't calm down she was going to make herself go into work and she really didn't feel like it.

As she sat on the sofa, sipping her coffee and looking out the bay window at the gray day, the doorbell rang. The sound made her jump and she was glad her coffee cup was empty.

"Mrs. Collins, it's Mrs. Malloy, she would like to speak to you if you will let her," Blanca announced.

"Of course, Blanca, show her in, thank you," Johnnie said.

Johnnie rose from her seat when Anna came into the room.

"Johnnie, thank you for seeing me," Anna said.

"Please join me, would you like some coffee? Blanca, please bring the coffee setup, you'll find it in the butler's pantry. Anna, please have a seat," Johnnie said.

Johnnie and Anna exchanged pleasantries while Blanca got the coffee ready. After Blanca left there was an uneasy silence. Johnnie felt fidgety, wondering why Anna was visiting her.

"Johnnie, I just have to talk to you," Anna began, finally breaking the silence. "I have to apologize for my behavior Wednesday night. You and Patrick are fine people and I wouldn't hurt you for the world. I was just so angry and upset I didn't think before I spoke. Please forgive me."

"Anna, I'm so glad you said that, it means so much to me," Johnnie said reaching over and taking her neighbor's hand.

Anna took a pretty handkerchief out of her pocket and dabbed her eyes while Johnnie used her tissue to dab her eyes. The ladies talked for a while longer about the whole unhappy adventure with Charles Defoe. Then Anna left and Johnnie was alone again; her mother was off with Aunt Rose and Uncle Pete visiting the Huntington Library.

"Mrs. Collins, there's a phone call for you from Mrs. Stevens," Blanca announced.

"Thanks, Blanca," Johnnie said as she hurried to the phone.

"Johnnie, how about lunch today? We've got a lot to catch up on," Barb blurted.

"Yes, that sounds good. Shall we go to the Bullocks' Tea Room? I'll drive, I can pick you up now if you're ready," Johnnie said.

"So, tell me about the meeting Wednesday night," Barb said in a gossipy tone once the ladies were seated and reading their menus.

"Have you heard about Charles Defoe?" Johnnie asked.

"No. Oh, tell me, please," Barb said.

Johnnie started with the story of their disastrous meeting Saturday at the Biltmore and how she and Patrick checked Charles Defoe's office and found it vacant. Then she told Barb about the visit from Lionel on Sunday before she finished with the miserable meeting Wednesday night.

"Johnnie, I can't believe all this. Charles seemed so up front and honest. His presentations were flawless. Look at how all those education people invested with him," Barb said.

"You and Stan didn't invest with him, Barb," Johnnie said.

"There's something I have to confess to you on the Q.T., Johnnie; it can't get back to Stan so don't tell Patrick," Barb said in a low voice.

"What is it, Barb?" Johnnie asked.

"We're broke, stony broke, no money, up against it. We've been eating weenies and beans for ages. Otherwise we would have been investing just like the rest of you," Barb whispered.

"Oh, Barb, I'm so sorry," Johnnie said with real concern on her face.

"It's all our own fault. You know Stan the bon vivant and I'm

165

right there with him. You know the volunteer work I'm doing at the school, well I'm really substituting and may even have to go back to teaching full-time. That's something I just don't want to do. We're really counting on the book that Patrick and Stan are writing and are so grateful that Patrick included Stan," Barb said.

"I hope the book works out, too," Johnnie sympathized.

"Say, why haven't I seen you at the country club? Aren't you still on the swim team?" Barb asked.

"Yes, I'm still on the team but now I am swimming first thing in the morning. Sometimes I even get there before the club is open. The swimming really starts my day out right," Johnnie said enthusiastically.

"I miss our meetings, Johnnie. It's good to have lunch with you today. I have something else to confess that you can't tell Patrick because Stan really can't ever know," Barb said in a very quiet voice.

What now? Johnnie was worried; the last confession had been like a blow to her stomach. This time she held her breath waiting to hear what Barb would say.

"Johnnie, I almost was unfaithful to my marriage. I don't know what came over me, but if Charles had stayed around a little longer we probably would have had an affair. We were so close to it. I'm ashamed of myself," Barb said softly.

Johnnie wasn't surprised really, because she had noticed her friend's interest in Charles was a little too animated.

"Barb, I think that all the pressure of your finances made you reckless and I'm glad nothing happened you would regret later," Johnnie said.

"It was great getting together, Johnnie. I just feel so much better," Barb said getting out of the car once they were back home.

"I enjoyed our visit too, Barb, and will never tell anyone your confessions, believe me. Take care, my friend," Johnnie said.

Johnnie could hardly believe the confessions Barb had made at lunch and felt exhausted from hearing them. She was resting in the family room when the doorbell rang. *Now what?* she thought. She got up and hurried toward the front door, not knowing if Blanca was in the house.

"Mrs. Collins, it's Mrs. Johnston to see you," Blanca said when she ran into Johnnie in the hallway. "She has her children with her."

"Oh, dear. Better show them into the family room. Then could you bring some juice and crackers? Thank you."

"Hello Lisa, Peter, and Cindy. Why don't we have Peter and Cindy sit here and Blanca will bring some juice and crackers while your mommy and I talk," Johnnie said trying to corral the toddlers.

"Johnnie, sorry to bother you but I just had to come over and talk to you. I, that is, Tom and I, want you and Patrick to know that we stand behind you on this investment thing. I just wish one of us had stood up and said so like George Hampton did, but we just sat in our seats distressed by all that was happening. I hope you will forgive us for sitting," Lisa said.

"Lisa, thank you for coming over. It means a lot to me. It did hurt me to have our neighbors turn on us but one of them came by this morning and that eased the pain. I wasn't sure if we could stay in the neighborhood but now I am feeling better about the whole thing," Johnnie said.

"Did Paul Critchen come by?" Lisa asked.

"No, it was Anna Malloy. I don't think Mr. Critchen will ever take back what he said. He probably believes that Lionel actually plotted to take his money and that we were in on the scam. Honestly, I can understand why he got divorced, I just don't see how he got to keep the kids," Johnnie said.

Little Peter and Cindy had started to make noises and were getting up from their seats so Lisa got up to leave.

"Guess the gang is ready to roll, so I will too. It was good to talk with you, Johnnie," Lisa said as she zipped Peter's coat.

That evening, Johnnie told Patrick about the visits from the neighbors and how much better she felt. She told him about the lunch with Barb but not what they talked about, though she didn't like keeping secrets from her husband. She gave him a big kiss when she finished telling him about her day, thankful that Barb's secrets weren't hers.

167

Thirty-six

Thursday already, Johnnie thought as she drove in to do some work at Aunt Rose's company. Last Thursday Barb made her confession, so maybe she would call and find out if she wanted to go out to dinner to see how she was doing, since Patrick and Stan would be working on their book. But first, she would need to get through another day with the miserable Bill Stern. *He was just being pig-headed,* she thought to herself and smiled thinking of him with a pig head.

Traffic was moving on Huntington Drive this morning, so she got to work not too late after swimming. She found a parking place and sighed. This was not going to be an easy day she knew. The team working on Bill Stern's proposal was going to present to Aunt Rose, Scott, and Bill this morning. Johnnie wanted to get a cup of strong coffee before the meeting, so she hurried.

"Mrs. Collins."

Johnnie turned, shaded her eyes against the bright sun, and saw Bill Stern hurrying to catch up with her. *What a way to start the day.*

"So, today we hear what the group has been working on. Wonder what they came up with," Bill said as he caught up to Johnnie.

"I know that the group worked very hard on your suggestions, Bill. I'm sure you'll be happy with their conclusions," Johnnie said as positively as she could.

"We'll just see about that," Bill remarked, holding the door open for Johnnie.

Johnnie quickly walked to her office, stopping only to ask Sarah if there was any coffee. Within moments, her assistant was back with a mug and a sweet roll.

"Mrs. Collins, you looked like you could use a little refreshment," Sarah said.

"Yes, I went swimming this morning before coming into work and have worked up an appetite. Thanks, Sarah," Johnnie said taking the cup and roll, wishing the coffee had a little Irish in it. There was nothing like meeting Mr. Stern in the parking lot to make one want something a little stronger than coffee.

Rose appeared in the doorway and dramatically collapsed into one of the chairs. "Johnnie, I think for the meeting this morning we should probably keep our comments to a minimum in front of Bill. I just think that will work out better. I really am worried about him; I know he has his mind set on big expansion plans. We should do some updating of our equipment but I just can't see a big us doing a big expansion. Or maybe I'm just getting old. I don't know."

Johnnie looked at her aunt and saw the worry on her face. Yes, Aunt Rose did look old, and tired too. *This is not good,* Johnnie thought. *We can't let the group or Bill see either of us looking defeated.*

"Aunt Rose, I know the group has worked hard to find a way to make both you and Bill happy. I've helped with some of the numbers and I think everything will be okay," Johnnie said.

"You're right, Johnnie. You're always so positive," Rose said, rising from her chair. "I guess I just needed to hear some positive words."

Johnnie saw that Aunt Rose did walk straighter and with a lighter step. She was still dreading the meeting. In her heart she knew Bill Stern would not be happy with the results and wondered how her aunt would feel if Bill decided to march out of the company. He had a good history with the company after having been there for so many years. He was a valuable employee, Johnnie knew, and Aunt Rose would not want to lose him but she also didn't want to do a great big expansion. Johnnie wondered how Scott felt about the whole thing and decided to ask him.

"Scott, got a minute?" Johnnie asked, poking her head in his office.

"Sure! Come on in, Mom," Scott said.

They talked about the meeting and their thoughts on it. Scott wanted to wait for the presentation before he made up his mind. He didn't really want to get into a big expansion while still trying to learn the business from Aunt Rose. But if the group made a compelling case, then he would consider it.

The meeting was worse than Johnnie could ever have imagined. The group got so frustrated with Bill that some of their voices got loud, too loud, in Johnnie's opinion. The presentation took much longer than it should have because Bill kept interrupting, until finally Aunt Rose asked him very patiently to let the talk go forward. When the meeting was over, Bill stormed out of the room before anyone else could even get out of their seats.

Very unpleasant meeting, Johnnie thought driving home; the traffic was heavier on Huntington, but at least it was moving. She was looking forward to dinner with Barb and wished her mother could join them, but she already knew she wouldn't. Johnnie wondered how her mother's always wanting to give them privacy would work out if she moved in with them as she started to drive again.

"Oh, it's good to see you, Barb," Johnnie said as they settled into a booth at Dobson's. Johnnie had decided she had a taste for Dobson's beef brochettes and Barb said she wanted some lobster so they agreed on the meet there. *I thought she was broke,* Johnnie thought snidely.

"Oh, I needed this," Johnnie said sipping her martini.

"Bad day?" Barb asked.

"No, just difficult personalities, that's all. How about you, Barb?" Johnnie said.

"I have tell you something more," Barb said, taking a good swig from her martini.

Not again, Johnnie thought as her hand gripped the stem of her glass tightly and her stomach tightened.

"It's not like last Thursday's confession, so you can let go of your death grip on your glass," Barb said laughing. It's just that I know the name of 'the Babe.' Charles Defoe knew her and she introduced Charles to Lionel, because as we know Lionel knows 'the Babe.' Anyway, her name is actually Lottie Martin. Seems Lottie and the Marshalls were at a party together and that's when Lottie introduced Charles."

Johnnie was stunned. She hadn't really thought about how Charles and Lionel got together, she'd assumed they met through Lionel's work connections. *Was Lottie Martin one of Lionel's work connections? And when they met, Linda was there?* It was a lot to think about, but she would have to do it later because she knew Barb would not want to even discuss it.

That night when Patrick was eating the snack Johnnie prepared for him, she now had a snack waiting for him every Thursday night because she knew he would come home hungry, she only told him about her work and kept the news about Lottie Martin to herself, not wanting to explain why Barb knew the name. Now she was keeping another secret from Patrick and didn't like herself for it.

Thirty-seven

As she tossed and turned all night long, Johnnie sighed and watched the clock tick off the hours. Between the meeting with Bill Stern and dinner with Barb, her mind wouldn't stop racing. *What did "the Babe" no, now she had a name, Lottie Martin, have to do with anything? Did Linda know her or what?* Johnnie had pulled out the list that she kept in her desk and wrote "Lottie Martin?" not knowing how she fit in but believing there was some kind of mysterious connection.

Finally it was time to get up. She rolled out of bed yawning and stretching.

"Are you all right? You really tossed and turned last night. Do you think you're coming down with something?" Patrick inquired politely, coming around from the other side of the bed and holding her.

"I'm okay, sweetie, just couldn't stop thinking about the meeting yesterday that's all. I know I'm being silly," Johnnie said quickly in hope of avoiding one of Patrick's concoctions this particular morning.

They both got dressed hurriedly since they woke up a little late. Johnnie had managed to sleep the last few hours, a deep restful sleep, so she didn't feel too bad. She decided she wouldn't go in to work today and chose some dark brown slacks and a coral sweater. She pinned her hair back at the neck with a tortoise shell barrette and since her ears were showing she put on some gold balls for earrings.

"Not going to work, my sweet?" Patrick asked with concern.

"Just don't feel like it. I'm going to spend some time with my mother," Johnnie said.

Johnnie still didn't want one of Patrick's concoctions, especially if he used raw egg. He always was ready with his drinks and she and the kids knew to be careful around him otherwise they would be given one. She loved him for wanting to make everyone okay, so she gave him a sweet kiss.

They walked arm and arm down the beautiful staircase through the foyer, turning left towards the breakfast room.

"Good morning, Johnnie and Patrick," Iris sang out. "Blanca prepared a wonderful breakfast this morning." Iris got up to leave.

"Mother, don't be silly! You don't have to leave now that we're here," Johnnie reproached her.

"I'm finished and you need time together," Iris said.

Johnnie sighed to herself. If her mother was going to live with them she would need to be less sensitive about interfering because she would be part of the family, but would she understand that? It would drive Johnnie crazy if her mother kept disappearing every time they came into the room.

"Oh, that was a good breakfast. Blanca's omelet was great. But now I must run. Sure you'll be okay?" Patrick said, leaning over and kissing Johnnie.

"Yes, I'm just fine. Will you be playing golf today?" Johnnie asked.

"No golf today, this afternoon Stan and I will be working. I just don't know," Patrick said.

"Well I do! I know you'll work something out with Stan. We've known him for a long time and Barb said he was very pleased you asked for his help," Johnnie said.

"Oh dear, I was afraid of that. Well, I just have to try," Patrick said with a deep sigh.

Johnnie stood up and kissed Patrick with feeling; she was so relieved to hear him say he wouldn't give up on Stan.

"Mmm...maybe I should call in sick today," Patrick teased, holding Johnnie and kissing her.

"No you go on to work, lover, and I will see you this afternoon," Johnnie said.

"It's a date," Patrick agreed, walking quickly out of the house with a spring in his step and whistling.

Johnnie returned to her seat and was reading the paper and drinking coffee when the phone rang.

"Mrs. Collins, there's a Lieutenant Olsen on the phone for either you or Mr. Collins," Blanca said breathlessly.

"It's okay, Blanca, I'll take it in my office," Johnnie said.

"Lieutenant Olsen, this is Mrs. Collins. Do you have news for us?"

"No, Mrs. Collins, I don't. I'd like to come over and talk to you to see if you remember anything else. I'm in the neighborhood and can be there in five minutes," Lieutenant Olsen said in a weary voice.

What is he doing in our neighborhood? Didn't he work in Los Angeles? Guess I'll find out soon enough. Her thoughts were interrupted when the doorbell rang. Her stomach lurched with the chimes. *Pull yourself together, Johnnie,* she told herself. *You've done nothing wrong.*

"Mrs. Collins, Lieutenant Olsen is here. Where do you want me to put him?" Blanca whispered.

"Take him to the living room and ask if he wants any coffee. I'll be there in a minute," Johnnie answered.

Johnnie ducked into the bathroom off the kitchen and checked her appearance. She smoothed her hair and straightened her sweater, which was a little messed up after saying goodbye to Patrick. She stood up straight and marched to the living room, telling herself, *I've done nothing wrong,* with each step. She pasted on a smile she hoped wasn't sick-looking and walked into the living room.

"Lieutenant Olsen," Johnnie said.

The lieutenant rose when Johnnie entered. She noticed he looked tired and, well, just plain beaten down.

"Sorry to bother you, Mrs. Collins, but I just haven't been able to get a hold of Mr. Marshall either at home or his office," Lieutenant Olsen said.

"Oh, I know Mr. Marshall is very busy. I don't think he's trying to avoid you. He lost money with Mr. Defoe, or whatever his name is, you know," Johnnie said quickly.

"I know that, Mrs. Collins, I just want to find out how Mr. Collins and Mr. Defoe got together that's all," Lieutenant Olsen said.

"Oh, if that's all I can tell you that," Johnnie blurted out before she could stop herself; she wanted desperately to clap her hand over her mouth.

"Do continue, Mrs. Collins," Lieutenant Olsen said leaning forward in his chair.

Oh dear, I can't get out of it now. I'll just try to leave Barb's name out of it. That's the least I can do, Johnnie thought.

"Lottie Martin introduced Charles Defoe to the Marshalls at a party that they all attended. It was there that Lionel made arrangements for the investment parties. That's all I know," Johnnie said.

"Thank you, Mrs. Collins, you've been very helpful," the lieutenant said as he jumped out of his seat and headed for the door. "I don't need to remind you not to discuss this case with anyone?"

Johnnie sat stunned in the living room, staring out the bay window and wondering just how she had been "so helpful." She couldn't discuss this meeting with Patrick and hoped her mother didn't know about it. Now she was keeping a secret of her own from Patrick and that made her sad.

Thirty-eight

"Johnnie, oh Johnnie," Iris called, walking into the living room. "I've been looking for you. Would you mind taking me to Hinshaw's this morning? I've seen something in the paper I want to get there."

"Oh Mother, of course not, I'd be delighted to take you. Do you want to go now?" Johnnie said.

Johnnie and her mother drove over to Arcadia and Hinshaw's. Her mother found what she wanted, but both ladies enjoyed shopping through the store as long as they were there. Johnnie was glad to have the distraction.

"Are you hungry, Mother? It's almost lunch time," Johnnie said.

"Yes, I am hungry. With all this shopping, I've worked up an appetite," Iris said.

Since they were in Arcadia, Johnnie took her mother to Van De Kamp's for a quick bite. She always liked going there because when her children were little they used to beg to go to the restaurant with the big windmill. She smiled as they walked by the big windmill and forgot all about her morning visitor.

When they got home, unloaded their packages, and Johnnie got her mother settled, she realized she hadn't gone swimming yet. *Well, she thought, there is time but I don't really want to. Maybe a little more activity on the Solo Flex will make up for a missed day. But I sure hope Coach Hank doesn't take role call!*

When Johnnie saw Patrick get out of the car she could tell he was beat. She hoped it wasn't because of Stan. She decided to go out and meet him with her brightest smile.

"Hi, honey. It's good to have you home again," Johnnie said squeezing Patrick's arm.

AN EVIL GROWS IN PASADENA

"Johnnie, I just don't know. I just don't know," Patrick replied, shaking his head.

Johnnie didn't let her smile droop and she squeezed Patrick's arm a little harder, reached up, and kissed him. She felt him relax, saw a tiny smile form on his lips, and felt a little hope that maybe he would keep working with Stan. She didn't know if Stan had told him they were broke and she didn't want to betray Barb's secret, but since Patrick kept working with him, she thought he probably knew.

Over cocktails he told Johnnie just how difficult it was working with Stan who was very detailed oriented, even more than Patrick. Johnnie couldn't believe that her husband was admitting to his detail fixation but said nothing and tried not to smile. As he told her about his day, she thought about her day and wondered how she would handle Lieutenant Olsen.

"So what did you ladies do today?" Patrick asked when he finally finished with his day.

"Well, Mom and I went shopping at Hinshaw's and then we had lunch at Van de Kamp's."

"Ah, the big windmill. Remember how the kids used to beg to go there?"

"I sure do. Patrick, I should tell you about the visitor we had before we left to go shopping. Lieutenant Olsen stopped by," Johnnie said.

"Did he find Charles?" Patrick said excitedly.

"No, he came over looking for Lionel, who apparently has not been available either at his home or his office. They still don't have any leads on where Charles might be. I don't think we'll see any of our money," Johnnie said.

"No, that money is gone. By the way, Lionel hasn't been playing golf with us either for the last couple of games. We've had to pick up a fourth at the course. Don't know what that's all about either," Patrick said thoughtfully.

They finished their cocktails in silence, looking out the bay window as the sun set. Johnnie felt all right with herself for not telling Patrick the whole truth about the lieutenant's visit, because he'd instructed her not to discuss the case firmly before he left.

After a good dinner of spaghetti and meatballs, garlic toast, and salad, Johnnie went up to exercise; Patrick retired to his study; and Iris went to her room to read, and probably went to bed. As Johnnie was exercising, Patrick came into the room.

"Johnnie, I forgot to tell you it's our turn to host the Superbowl party this year," Patrick announced.

"When is the Superbowl and who are the teams?" Johnnie panted between reps.

"It's January twenty-fifth, between the Raiders and the Philadelphia Eagles," Patrick said wringing his hands.

"There's plenty of time to organize the party, Patrick, and mother and Blanca will help me. Don't worry about it, we ladies will have everything under control," Johnnie said climbing off the Solo Flex and blotting her face and body with a towel just in case Patrick decided to get physical.

Thirty-nine

Johnnie woke slowly as the sun played on her eyes, then she closed them tightly realizing it was Monday, and she just wanted to pull the covers over her head. The weekend had been so much fun once Ian had unexpectedly come home from Occidental College. It had been a nice treat for all of them, but now she would have to face work and the petulant Bill Stern. *No,* she thought. *I have the Superbowl party to plan and Blanca will be home this morning and so will Mother. No, I'm not going in to work today.* With that settled, Johnnie turned over to go back to sleep.

"Hey, sleepy-head, rise and shine. It's Monday, time to start all over again," Patrick said stripping the covers off the bed.

Johnnie got up, stretched and gave her husband a kiss.

"Nope, I'm not going to the office today. There's too much to do here at home," Johnnie told him as she straightened his tie.

Patrick hugged his wife and caressed her, giving a final sweet kiss before leaving for work. Johnnie then took a quick shower, got dressed in comfortable slacks and a sweater, and went down the back stairs. After a simple breakfast, Johnnie gathered the women around the kitchen table.

"Ladies, we're to have the group over for the Superbowl Sunday game this year," Johnnie declared.

"Oh, it should be a good game. The Raiders are a wild card team and they'll be playing the Philadelphia Eagles. Wild card teams don't usually make it all the way so it should be interesting," Blanca said enthusiastically.

Johnnie and her mother looked at Blanca blankly. Neither of them followed football.

J. ROSWELL

"The game will be in the Superdome in New Orleans this year," Blanca continued.

"If the game is going to be in New Orleans, let's do a Southern theme," Iris said.

"That should be fun, Mom. Do you know the colors of the teams, Blanca? Or maybe we should just do the Raiders colors, because don't they come from California?"

"The Raiders are from Oakland and they wear silver and black," Blanca said.

"Oh, if we're doing anything Southern, we'll have to have fried chicken. And I want to make a chess pie," Iris said.

Johnnie thought about Linda as they pored over cookbooks, discussing various recipes. She wondered if her friend was back in town yet and if Linda would call when she got here. Would she be with Lionel or would it be "the Babe," as Johnnie still called Lottie Martin, thinking it fit her better. Speaking of Lionel, she hoped this party would go better with him than the last one when he was hostile because she had used Linda's recipes. Johnnie still hadn't worked out in her mind what his strange reaction meant, if anything. She decided after a while to go swimming and left her mother and Blanca still looking through the cookbooks.

Driving home after a great swim where Coach Hank had praised her, saying she was really becoming a strong swimmer and great addition to the team, she smiled and hummed to herself. Yes, the workouts in the pool and on the Solo Flex were bothersome sometimes, but they were paying off and she was glad she decided to join the team.

Forty

Johnnie shifted and rolled in bed, trying very hard not to disturb Patrick. She wondered if her mother was sleeping all right over at Aunt Rose's. The weather had picked up that afternoon with a strong, cold northern wind that was bringing in another rainstorm. The wind was whistling and howling around the house, making the pyracantha bush on the south side of the house bang and scrape against the first floor windows. She really must get Henry to trim the bush back even with its sharp thorns and the sooner the better. She could hear an occasional desperate dog bark and someone's wind chimes were madly clanging.

The room was so dark she couldn't see her hand in front of her face. The moon and starlight that usually lit their bedroom were covered by dark clouds. The house creaked and cracked even more, and the windows rattled in the wind, making Johnnie shiver. *I'm just as bad as the kids,* she thought, *it's only the wind pull yourself together.*

She was greatly relieved when the sun finally hauled its way above the horizon. She yawned and stretched, climbed out of bed slowly stretching some more. She grabbed her quilted bathrobe off a nearby chair, snuggled into it, and put on her warm fuzzy sleepers. *The house is so cold on winter mornings,* she thought, *it would be good to have a fire.* Then she started wondering why the original owners had built only one fireplace in the library of the house. *I wonder how difficult it would be to have one added to the bedroom?*

But for this morning, Patrick had already left for the university so she just moved the thermostat up just a little. They really didn't keep their house very warm, they chose to wear warm clothes instead, but it was very cold this morning. Johnnie laughed to herself, thinking of Larry and Carol in New York. They probably would consider Pasadena's weather a heat wave. But it did feel cold enough to snow.

Patrick was gone, her mother was with Aunt Rose, and Blanca would be leaving for school soon. She was looking forward to being alone in the house for a while; she would use the time to make her Superbowl plans final, it was already Friday, and she wanted to be perfectly ready. This was an important occasion for her, not the game but the party, all the women tried to out-do each other for the Superbowl game. The group included Patrick's golfing buddies, and Stan and Barb. The golfers included Lionel and she wondered again if he would come, and if Linda would be with him or would Lottie Martin be his guest. When would Linda be back? Her Christmas letter said soon but that didn't really tell her anything.

She walked to her dressing room stopping at the tall dresser to look at her children and nephews. Johnnie dressed in slacks, a turtleneck, and her warmest sweater, buttoning the cardigan up to her neck. Then she waltzed down the back stairs humming happily because for the moment it was quiet outside. The blasted wind had died, which was great even though she knew that was only temporary and there would probably be the heavy rain that was predicted.

"Mrs. Collins, I've got breakfast for you then I've got to run class you know," Blanca said on seeing Johnnie.

"Yes, I know you've got to leave. I'm going to be working on the Superbowl party this morning while the house is quiet. Mother will be coming back this afternoon and so will Patrick. No golf for him today, not with this weather," Johnnie said as she sipped her coffee.

After Blanca left and the kitchen was cleaned and shining, Johnnie retired to her office off the kitchen. She sat at her desk going over her notes and tapping her pencil. She really needed to take an inventory of Patrick's wines. She sighed as she looked across the desk at the shelves holding the wine. Patrick always counted on her for this inventory but the wine was on the north wall and it was cold over there. She sat tapping her pencil and sipping her coffee staring at the wine. A strange buzzing brought her out of her daydreams with a start and she spilled a little of her coffee as her hand jerked. Then she realized it was the buzzer outside the kitchen.

Who the devil is ringing that bell? We aren't expecting any deliveries, and Pearl and her girls aren't expected. I suppose it could be Henry, she thought getting up to answer the annoying buzzing. Johnnie briskly walked the short distance to the door, standing straight ready to deal with who ever was making so much noise. She threw open the door with a flourish trying at the last minute not to bang the wall.

"Oh, Johnnie, sorry to disturb you," Lionel said.

Lionel stood there with his left hand resting on the kitchen wall close to the bell, looking disheveled, certainly not as crisp as he normally was. His hair was blown by gusts of wind, he had dark circles under his eyes, and his face was pale, very pale. His clothes were not of his usual high standard and seemed rumpled, maybe not even clean. Johnnie was startled, first by Lionel ringing the kitchen doorbell and then by his appearance.

"Lionel, what brings you to my kitchen door?" Johnnie asked once she got over the shock of seeing him there.

"I need to borrow your man. A tree fell last night blocking my access to the backyard. Unfortunately, my gardener isn't due until Monday and won't be available to help with this emergency. How did your yard fare?" Lionel said in a weary voice.

He sounds as bad as like he looks...maybe he didn't sleep any better than I did. She motioned Lionel in then went to the intercom to find Henry.

"Henry, would you come up to the house," Johnnie said into the intercom once she found him in the garage.

"I'll be right up, Mrs. Collins," Henry answered in an electronic voice.

Lionel stood to the side looking dejected while Johnnie was trying to find Henry. *Really he is a sight, if Linda were here she would be taking care of the tree and she wouldn't be asking me to help with it,* Johnnie thought bitterly.

"Henry, how is our yard after that big wind last night?" Johnnie asked when Henry came into the house.

"There's a lot of clean up of leaves and such to be done. Nothing is down though," Henry said.

"That's good for us, but Mr. Marshall needs help with a tree that fell in his backyard and is blocking his access. Would you be able to help him?" Johnnie asked.

"I think so, but I'll have to see what needs to be done," Henry answered.

Johnnie grabbed her warm jacket off the hook by the door, decided on her scarf also, and hoped there were gloves in the jacket pockets. There were bursts of cold wind and it was dark and threatening rain. She shivered as she opened the door, stepping out into a gust of a brisk wind that made her scarf flutter.

The three of them walked quickly to Lionel's home with the cold wind swirling around them and throwing a few raindrops on them as they made their way. Johnnie put the gloves from her pockets on with resentment, not really wanting to share Henry with Lionel.

"Okay, so here's the problem as you can see. This big tree uprooted in the wind and blocked the passage to the rest of the yard unless I want to swim my way through. At least the tree didn't go into the pool. I just want Henry to cut the tree back up by the garage so there will be a pathway then I can have my regulars do the rest. I sure appreciate the help," Lionel said pointing to the fallen tree.

"What about lightning with rain about to come? I really don't want Henry doing much here with this bad weather," Johnnie said after seeing the hopeless mess before them.

"I think I can get a small pathway done fairly quickly, Mrs. Collins," Henry volunteered, studying the tree.

"Let me get some tools from the garage," Lionel said.

Johnnie followed Lionel and peered into the garage as he opened the door.

"Is Linda home?" Johnnie asked on seeing Linda's car with the distinctive license plate 4LMLLM.

Lionel slammed the garage door down and turned on Johnnie. "No, she isn't here," he barked.

For just a second Johnnie knew that Linda was never going to come back because she was dead by Lionel's hand. She recovered herself quickly and pasted a pleasant smile on her face, hoping Lionel didn't know what she was thinking. She wanted to run home, taking Henry with her and locking all the doors but that would let Lionel know she suspected him so she moved slowly.

"I think Henry has an idea how to handle your problem so guess I'll head home, Lionel," Johnnie said as lightly as she could.

She turned and walked at a normal pace out of Lionel's backyard while he went to help get Henry started. Once out on the street she picked up her pace, finally running to her kitchen door. Inside she locked the door firmly, not worrying about the rest of the doors because she knew they were all locked.

Forty-one

Seated at her desk, Johnnie pulled out her list and added Linda's car. She studied the list: Linda's disappearance; missed appointments, especially the LaBauch appointment; recipes left behind; Christmas letter with potatoes from Perris; Lottie Martin; and finally Linda's car. *What would Lt. Olsen think of this list?* Barb would probably laugh if she told her that she knew immediately when she saw Linda's car that their friend was no longer alive. *But what can I do about it? Would anyone believe me?*

Deep in thought, Johnnie started the inventory of the wine for Patrick. The wind was blowing again outside and she hoped Henry wouldn't be at Lionel's very long for more than one reason. How could Lionel have done that to Linda, she was such a great person, a loving wife, and a wonderful friend. *Linda thought the world of that creep,* she thought bitterly. The house was moaning and creaking and the windows were rattling, adding to her bleak mood.

She worked for a while and finally reached the bottom back area where Patrick kept his most expensive wines. They were all still on the shelf she was sure, but she would carefully check each bottle off the list so Patrick would know she had checked. She had to bend over in a crouch to reach the shelf and it was awkward. She wanted to hurry because she was uncomfortable in her crouching position.

She stopped, even as she felt like her legs were cramping, because she thought she heard glass breaking. Her heart started racing and she was holding her breath. *Oh, silly girl, it's probably just some wind chime you're hearing. Get back to work.* She sighed and continued looking at the wine bottles.

She stood, stretched, placed the list on the file cabinet, and took a deep breath, raising her head and chest up. As she brought her head and chest back down, she noticed a man's shoe at the corner of the desk.

Her heart pounded in her ears so loudly she couldn't hear as she quickly grabbed a wine bottle and hid it behind her before she checked any further. Then she turned and looked quickly at the desk. Lionel stood at the corner of the desk, his hair covered his forehead, his dark eyes looked like coal, his grim lips were purple, and his cheeks flushed ruddy. In his hand was Johnnie's scarf.

"Johnnie, you are so beautiful, why did you have to mess in my business? You are just so beautiful, how can I do what I must do?" Lionel muttered in a low hostile voice.

Johnnie, with a quick motion, brought her wine bottle down on Lionel's knee as hard as she could.

"Oh, owwww," Lionel cried in pain, falling to the floor at Johnnie's feet. "How could you do that to me?"

"This is for Linda," Johnnie said and bopped his shoulder.

Then she climbed easily over the desk, grateful for all the days and hours on the Solo Flex and in the swimming pool. She ran down the short hall to the kitchen door, still carrying the wine bottle tightly in her hand. She threw open the door Lionel had left unlocked after breaking in.

Running outside in a blind panic, she felt someone grab her arm and heard an ear-piercing scream that just didn't seem to stop; it was hurting her ears. Someone yanked the wine out of her hand. She could feel herself being laid down and she struggled fiercely, then she felt a prick in her arm and everything went dark.

Forty-two

Johnnie awoke slowly, not at all sure where she was. She thought maybe she was in her old house and pictured the room the way her other bedroom had been. She rolled and sighed. She could hear a heavy rain beating against the windows and didn't know what time of day it was and she wasn't in her pajamas but in clothes in bed.

"Johnnie, are you awake?" Barb said in a very soft voice.

What was Barb doing here? Johnnie thought. *Surely, we're not vacationing together and I forgot.*

"Barb?" Johnnie said rising up slowly.

"Let me help you, Johnnie. Do you want me to get Patrick?" Barb leaned down and helped Johnnie out of bed.

"No, not right now. I want to clean up first," Johnnie said slowly as the morning's adventure started to set in along with a heavy feeling of dread.

The ladies walked arm in arm past the tall dresser and Johnnie waved to her pictures as they passed.

"We've been taking turns keeping watch over you. Everyone is so worried about you, Johnnie. No one can believe what happened this morning—not our neighborhood, not such an evil growing right here in Pasadena on our street," Barb said as they made their way slowly.

Johnnie looked puzzled and felt very confused.

"Barb, why was I in bed with my clothes on?" Johnnie asked.

"You probably don't remember because you were given a sedative to calm you down. Lionel broke into your house with the plan to kill you. I'm just so glad he didn't succeed," Barb said with tears in her eyes.

"Oh, I am too, Barb. I remember I came from his house and knew he had killed Linda. Then the next thing I knew he was standing in my office with my scarf in his hand. I was lucky to be by the wine at the time. I sure hope I didn't use Patrick's most expensive bottle," Johnnie said.

"Don't worry about that, Johnnie. I'm sure Patrick would have given his entire wine collection and much more to keep you safe. I'm just amazed about your strength. Don't know if I could disable a man like you did; you really are a super woman," Barb said.

"It's all the swimming and the Solo Flex workouts…otherwise I probably would be on the floor of the office right now," Johnnie said. "Now I'm going to take a shower so would you wait for me in the dressing room?" Johnnie asked.

"Of course," Barb said.

When Johnnie got out of the shower and came into the dressing room she saw that Barb had been busy and most of her wardrobe was hanging outside the closet in any place Barb could find.

"Oh," Johnnie said.

"Yes, I brought your clothes out trying to pick something out for you to wear, a lot of neighbors are downstairs as well as your Aunt Rose, Ian, and Scott. I want you to look your prettiest," Barb said blushing. "I think this dress would be just right."

Barb was holding up a long dress with a paisley print in mauves and pinks. The dress had long sleeves and a rolled collar. Johnnie put the dress on and it hung on her.

"That's okay, Barb, I think I'll wear a pants outfit with a sweater. The winter white one will be good. It's all the swimming I've been doing lately. I may have to replace my wardrobe."

Johnnie dressed quickly then fixed her hair in an upsweep. She decided on gold knot earrings. Then she carefully took out a heart shaped locket from her jewelry box and held it tightly for a minute.

"What a beautiful locket!" Barb said.

"Patrick and the children gave it to me about ten years ago for Mother's Day," Johnnie explained as she carefully opened the locket. "Look how young everyone is; Ian was still in grammar school."

189

As Barb looked at the pictures, she told Johnnie that Lottie Martin was arrested for cocaine trafficking and was Lionel's source for cocaine, not his lover. According to Lionel, he never intended to kill Linda, it was an accident during a heated discussion about his cocaine use.

"But why were the police there?" Johnnie asked.

"Well, Henry was to fix Lionel's tree as you know. He came back to get some other tools because he couldn't find Lionel to get them from him. When he got back here, he saw Lionel breaking into your house, and ran fast as he could up to his apartment and called 911. Did you know that you really screamed when you came out of the house? I think they could hear you in San Diego. That's why you were given a sedative to calm you down," Barb said.

"Cocaine is such an evil. I don't think Lionel realized just what a dangerous path he was on and it cost him his wife, his success, his place in the community, and, hopefully, his freedom," Johnnie said as they slowly walked down the beautiful stairs through the hallways to the library.

They could hear a soft murmur of voices and they caught the homey scent of the fireplace as they approached the library. Johnnie clutched Barb's hand as they got closer to the door.

"Don't worry, Johnnie, everyone is a friend in there," Barb said squeezing her friend's hand back.

Johnnie straightened herself and put on what she hoped was a soft smile and not a grimace and walked on.

"Look who I've got," Barb sang out nice and loud.

Patrick rushed to the door to collect his wife, giving Johnnie a big hug and kiss right in front of everyone.

"Johnnie, Johnnie," Patrick whispered softly.

"Patrick," Johnnie said squeezing him back.

The couple walked slowly to the sofa, greeting everyone on the way.

"Can't believe that Lionel tried that, but sure glad you're still here," Dr. Tom said taking her hand and patting it.

Scott and Ian stood behind their mother taking turns rubbing her shoulders and Patrick held her close to him as if he was trying to keep her safe. Other neighbors came up to Johnnie: Stan, Anna Malloy, and the Carmichaels.

"Rose went to call Bill to tell him you're okay. He's been calling every hour. And I called Colleen and Larry and told them you would call them when you're able," Iris whispered.

Johnnie noticed that the library table had been moved to the far end of the room and had the entire menu for the Superbowl Sunday party laid out on it. Johnnie smiled to herself knowing it was her mother's doing. She always cooked when she was upset.

Johnnie sat back in her seat, felt so loved, closed her eyes, and then she said a prayer for Linda.

Postscript

Johnnie sent Blanca to replace the groceries for the Superbowl party and they went ahead with it. The Raiders won: twenty-seven to Philadelphia's ten. The Raiders were the first wild card team to win a Superbowl. The ladies planned a memorial for Linda while the men watched the game.

Charles Defoe was still missing and most of the investors did not expect to get back any of their money.

Lionel Marshall was taken to the prison hospital ward and was busy with Paul Graham planning his defense.

Recipe from the Old Recipe Cards

Deviled Crab

6 Tablespoons Butter
1 Cup Fresh Bread Crumbs
2 Tablespoons All Purpose Flour
1 Cup Milk
2 Hard Cooked Eggs Forced through a Sieve
2 Tablespoons of Minced Onion
2 Tablespoons of Minced Celery
1 Tablespoon of Fresh Lemon Juice
1 Teaspoon Dry Mustard
1 Teaspoon of Worcestershire Sauce
Cayenne Pepper to Taste
1 Teaspoon of Salt
Pepper to Taste
1 Pound Fresh Cooked Crab Meat Carefully Checked for Shells

In a heavy ten to twelve inch skillet, melt three tablespoons of butter, add the fresh breadcrumbs, toss in butter till lightly browned. Scrape into a bowl and set aside.

Melt the remaining three tablespoons of butter. Remove from heat, stir in flour, and blend until smooth. In a small saucepan bring milk to an almost simmer then add to the flour mixture, stirring constantly. When mixture is completely smooth, return to heat stirring constantly, bring to a boil, and cook one minute. Remove from heat and add hard cooked eggs, onions, celery, and seasonings. Taste and adjust seasonings. Fold in crabmeat.

Turn into a well-buttered dish nine inches across or into well-buttered individual shells and top with reserved crumbs. Bake in a preheated oven of 450 degrees for twelve to eighteen minutes, or until bubbling and nicely browned on top. Serve immediately.

May be made up to twenty-four hours ahead of time. Cover with plastic wrap and refrigerate. Add three to five minutes to the baking time if taken straight from refrigerator to oven.

Four Main Course or Six to Eight First Course Servings

Printed in the United States
20808LVS00002B/329